The Witch of Gormire

Ophelia Finsen

The Yorkshire Saga

The Witch of Gormire
-
Hob Hurst's House
Hob Hurst's Daughter
Hob Hurst's Legacy
Lost Children
The Geologist's Wife

ISBN: 978-1-9193695-0-1

Merel, who listened to my chatter of Abigail Craister, and liked the idea of Abigail being reabsorbed by nature after her great jump from Whitestone Cliff.

CHILDHOOD

The Early 1600s
Yorkshire
Northern England

"Everything is transient."

She took the young girl's hand and pushed it down into the dark, loamy earth. Fingers splayed, she watched the moist soil seep into the cracks across her knuckles, softening the callouses on her palms, creeping up under her fingernails to draw a territorial line against the creamy pink. It formed an arched line, like a sunrise on the horizon. An earthrise. This is our land. We are of it. It is of us.

"We all come from this. We all return to it."

The girl stared wide eyed at her grandmother, seemingly horrified that her death was already been spoken of. She was just past seven. Having survived the myriad of childhood diseases and traps – accident and cold, starvation and malnutrition – hopes were increasing that she would reach adulthood. Serve well. Her community. Her husband, when the time came. Her future children.

The old woman chuckled at the child's gravity. "Come, we'll away to the heather to sit. Keep out of the way of the horses."

She had come for the girl early in the morning. In the gloaming, as cats were shifting sulkily, the chickens were beginning to scratch. Birds were thinking of the morning chorus. The women were already up and away at the chores, the never ending toil of the household and family.

Hand in hand two generations separated by a housewife had left the village. They'd walked out past meadows and tended farmland and entered the forest. It was still damp with the night's rainfall. The ground was thick with ferns and bracken, lichen encrusted trees, mosses and the gently rotting scent of natural mulch. Fungi were beginning to strain, bursting forth from the undergrowth, splashes of vivid colours, jewels of the strange underground.

The girl of seven and the old woman nearing sixty had followed an age-old dirt track up through the forest, up the steep banks towards the moorland tops at the edge of the world's horizon. The views up here stretched out for fathoms. On clear days one could see the Pennines, the backbone of the country. So she was told. She wondered what bony structures might be out there, supporting the King's nation. And if those hills that she could never quite see were the backbone, what were their own moors? What vital part of the organism were they?

Up on the tops horses ran in the open grassland. The two figures skirted the edges, following tracts of heather moorland and copses of trees. They came to the cliff edge where they could stand and survey the Mowbray valley. Sitting down in rough, springy cushions of heather, the flowers now past their best, the two took some bread and felt the breeze through their hair. This was a frequent ritual for the old woman and child, but not a given for every family member. The grandmother had seen something of a kindred in the eyes of the sixth grandchild, even when she was just a little screaming baby. The excursions would not last all that longer, for a post had been found for the girl, and she was being sent away to work. Not all that far, certainly a distance that could be walked. But far enough to put some distance from the family home. Grandmother did not speak of it to the children, for fear of frightening them, or worse, encouraging rumours, but something dark was coming. It had already been building. The taint of association could kill. So it was she who had suggested the girl ought to be sent into service now.

The girl chewed on her bread, looking thoughtfully out across the neverending land. Then to the north, on the level of the clifftops. She pointed. "What's that way?"

"To the north?"

"Yes."

They had never walked much further north than where they now sat. Sometimes they never even came to the hilltops, but walked about the villages and forests lower down. Past by old abbey ruins, torn down by a change in the religious ways by an old king. Past a silent, still lake.

"More moorland," her grandmother said. "The high moors. The dark moors. Drovers roads and miles of nothing but the horizon. Keep over that way and you get to Osmotherley. I have a cousin near there. Perhaps you and I will walk that way one time."

"But I have to go to work soon," the girl said sulkily.

"Ah, you'll get a break sometime, we'll find a way."

A distant shout went up, and both looked back inland to see the riders galloping the horses. It was good land for horses, for the races, and a popular point for folk to come and watch in racing season. The vibration of the hooves thudded through the very earth, a vague rumble that reached them. "Horses have always run here. The memory of their hooves have been drummed into the bedrock," Grandmother muttered as she turned her back and looked once again out from the cliffs. "They run so fast you might think they'd burst out of the cliffs at our feet here."

"The horses?" the girl raised her eyebrows, not convinced. She leaned forward a little. Not that they could see the crumbling, rocky cliff face from where they sat.

"The memory of the races, I mean." Grandmother finished her bread and brushed the crumbs from her skirt. "Come now. We'll walk down to the lake and back around that way."

The north side of the lake was a steep fall of land dropping down from the base of the sharp rock face. The cliffs were soft, and boulders, loosened by storms, lay dead in the forest. Now set with new births of moss patches, the undergrowth creeping up around them as shrouds. To the south of the lake the ground was boggy, and open meadow land scattered with rushes and sparse copses of trees. A farmstead in the distance sat on the crest of a rolling hill. The lake was in a slight bowl of land, an ethereal and still mirror of water reflecting the sky. Seemingly neither fed nor feeding, for no river or stream that could be seen entered or departed from the body of water. Waterfowl darted in and out of water reeds, wide-splayed footed moorhens tapped their way over lillypads as if they could walk on water. Fish roamed in the unknown depths, smaller ones eaten by grebes and diving ducks; larger ones taken out by the large Osprey that would fly overhead in spring, passing through for nesting places further north.

The girl could not take her eyes from the water as they walked by, trusting in the guiding hand of her grandmother. They moved along the shoreline, skirting rushes and hummocks of grass, avoiding the boggiest parts. The land was not too wet yet, but the autumn rains would soon come, followed by winter, then it would return to its mire state as harked in the lake's name: Gormire.

There were old stories her grandmother had told her about the place. Of the village that had once been there, long since submerged after terrible floods. If you listened very carefully, it was sometimes possible to hear the church bell ringing. Tales of a worm like beast, twisted up in the underbelly of the waters. Some said the lake was so deep that one would fall out of the earth if one fell in, and that that water was pouring out of the bottom of the world. Others said there was a tunnel, that ran for miles from the lake and popped up again in a spring nine miles away. No one was ever sure exactly where the exit was, only that it was precisely nine miles from the centre of Gormire.

One of her favourite tales was about the devil, when grandmother was in the mood for embellishing her stories, and would tell it with wide eyes and an orchestra of arm movements. It was said that the devil was riding his horse up on the cliff tops. He had lost control of the horse and they had leapt from the cliff and come crashing down to land. Such a crater had been formed from the impact, which filled when the winter rains and snow came. Grandmother didn't like to tell that tale anymore. There was more talk of the devil than ever. When it started, the wise would lower their eyes and merge into the background. They were not bad, only too worldly wise to understand loose tongues relishing in made up stories of devilry were now in a position to blame everyone and anything for their misfortune. Which was as it always had been, only with the new king there were now officials who took stories of devilish behaviour seriously. They looked out for the evil one's agents, so better to pluck them from society and exterminate them. It was a bad age to stand out or be noticed.

Grandmother had always seen that spark in the girl's eyes. Originally she had been pleased to see the family line appearing in the next generation. Now it worried her, and she advised her daughter to spread the energy far apart, in the hope that it would not be noticed. She herself was becoming more silent, less helpful in the community. She avoided conversation and advice, melted to the shadows, and soon people forgot to ask her for help, no longer quizzing her knowledge of the old ways. She grew towards a harmless old woman. Locals turned to the daughter, who was too full of compassion to acknowledge she could not fix all the woes in the world. One day someone would blame her.

In recent years women were being viewed more like children. To be in the background to work but not to trouble the adults with their voices nor their opinions. For they were too simple minded and easily led to have anything worth saying. That is what she had heard the new priest at Coxwold saying. Grandmother had felt something cold flash over her grave. She had heard the king had a paranoia of evil, of things he could not control that might have power over him. And he meant to rid his kingdoms of such things. The sickness spread out from the courts and the churches, a black sickness that was poisoning people's minds.

She could not talk sense into her daughter. She couldn't believe things would get so bad. Her eyes darted to the top of her granddaughter's dark chestnut waves. They ought to get her cap on before they reached the village. She ought to look the part of the pious little maid. She hoped she could hide her, keep her safe in plain sight until the worst of this era had passed by.

"Mary, where are you?"

The girl was hunched up in a corner, knees tucked under chin and resting having scoured a large cooking pot. She was oblivious to the name being called. Her child eyes gazed out of the open scullery door, watching the maid Martha beating dust out of a small rug from her lady's parlour. To the casual eye, it was the same action as every week, but the young girl watched the angle of the back, or perhaps it wasn't anything as obvious at that, just a mere nuance. But she knew that Martha was with child. Martha, the unmarried house maid, only fourteen years old. Who didn't have a sweetheart.

"Mary, Mary, where are you hiding? I have a chicken here that needs plucking. Get on with you." The cook, Mrs Cook, bustled into the room and halted, speechless for a moment as she caught sight of Mary gazing out of open door. She opened her mouth to begin scolding, but noted that the lass had made a good job of cleaning out the pot. A lot better than the previous little kitchen maid had managed. Not that one could really blame the girl – although the mistress of the house did – for she'd come to them ill, with bloodied lungs, and hadn't lived past the winter.

"Mary?"

The girl twisted and stared innocently up at Mrs Cook, with a question of 'who' in the rounded shape of her lips.

"You. Your name is Mary, remember?"

"No, it's..."

Mrs Cook hushed her. "I know you were christened Abigail, but here your name is Mary. You know none of us staff go by our real names."

"Why?"

"Because it makes life easier for our masters and mistresses. With staff changing, they don't need to remember new names." Mrs Cook, real name widow Anne Thwaite, had taken a great many months to grow accustomed to the demands of the household. Her own experience gave her more patience with the young maids and stableboys that came into employ, when they struggled with the concept of a new name, that their own identity meant nothing here. They all grew to accept it with time.

"They'll have to learn a new name when Martha's baby comes."

Mrs Cook gagged on horror. "What are you talking about? It's wicked to tell lies."

"But she is with child."

She looked at Martha, who had been looking a little wan recently, but still stubbornly continuing with her work. With child? Could it be so? There was no obvious sign, and she couldn't imagine that Martha would have confided such a thing to a little girl such as Abigail-Mary. "How do you...." she didn't bother to finish her question, Abigail's parentage coming to mind. "But you're Kerenza Craister's daughter, aren't you?" she said for no one's benefit, thinking of the midwife of Kilburn. "I imagine you're as canny as she is."

Abigail blushed and looked at the floor. "Grandmother says I'm not to talk of it."

"And that's the first sensible thing I've heard out of your mouth today. Now, don't you dare breath a word about babies to anyone, you hear? Even a mere hint like that can cause all kinds of trouble."

Abigail nodded meekly. "Do you think she'll marry and move away?"

Mrs Cook's face creased in concern. She'd been in service here ten years, and given the turnover of young maids finding themselves in the family way, she doubted it. Always leaving with the burden of shame on their backs. She had hoped age and time would have lessened the need, and indeed, Martha had managed three years here with no bother. Mrs Cook had dared to hope things were better now. Perhaps not. She herself had not noticed any outward signs of pregnancy on Martha, but once the seed was planted, it took root and she couldn't stop searching for signs, her gaze lingering on Martha a little too long. The girl noticed, and grew more clumsy under the observation.

The question was dealt with one evening in the yard out of the scullery, when Mrs Cook went out and found Martha sorting a basket of freshly laundered linens. Their washerwoman, Bessie had left the basket in the yard before heading home to begin afresh with all of her other chores, the ones that went unpaid but were held closer to her heart. The Angehards didn't like to have too many live in staff, for fear the lower class would eat them out of house and home.

Mrs Cook made certain there was no one else about, and for the most part she was thorough, only that she had not noticed Abigail-Mary who was crouched in the woodshed playing with a rat she'd been taming the past week. She sidled up to Martha as if she were about to indulge in great gossip. Martha looked up fearful. Cook couldn't make out yet whether it was because she was worried Cook knew her secret, or she was concerned all this attention meant displeasure about her work.

Mrs Cook nodded to her.

"Bessie just brought the linens in."

"I don't know how to phrase this," Mrs Cook started, conscious that this conversation had a limited time slot. She couldn't let anyone overhear, for if Mary was wrong, and rumours started, the girl could be ruined for no good reason. "Mary mentioned something and it's got me worrying. I have to ask, are you with..."

"There's only me here just now. I've not been sneaking off!" Martha protested.

"No, I mean, are you with..." She couldn't bring herself even to voice such an innocent word as child. That such a word could be so heavily loaded with accusation and shame. Instead she meaningfully nodded in the direction of Martha's stomach. She might have wondered if she was still to be misunderstood, but Martha coloured violently, the blush rushing up her neck, spreading over her face and making her ears burn. Mrs Cook closed her eyes. Not again.

"How did you..." Martha whispered hoarsely. "You can't tell can you?"

A great many housekeepers would have preached the Lord's good word at this point, slapped the girl and dismissed her immediately in her shame. A harlot at best, and in the current climate of witch chatter, she would be at risk of other accusations if she tried to drag the wrong man, the father, into the situation. Mrs Cook had lived through a lot of hardship, both personally and from the sidelines. It had been drummed into her since birth that women were subservient to men, that they were there only to make a man's life better. Women were dumb, incapable, and needed the business of repetitive simple chores to keep them out of mischief. A sentiment that was increasing, and yet with the years, Mrs Cook had started to wonder, was it so? She'd seen far too many maids preyed upon by their lords and masters, only to be denied and cast out when the inevitable happened. It was as if once they had left the employ of the hall, they ceased to exist. They merely evaporated into the background, and there was no problem, no culpability, no consequence. Those girls had known the risk, and most of them had not wanted to comply, but what chance did some of such low status, and a woman to add to it all, have? If women were so stupid, ought not the lord and master take care of them. As a guardian?

Women were not stupid. She'd seen them drag themselves and their families through all kinds of hardship. Through illness, through birthing, through bad harvests, poverty, rents they could barely afford to pay. Raising the new generation of labourers to be poorly paid to keep the lords and masters in their comfortable homes. Mrs Cook had gone through her own tragedies only to be told it was the Lord's way and no less than she deserved. She had started to look and to think. And found compassion for the chance of life that affected everyone.

"No one can tell yet," she spoke to Martha. "But they will soon. You need to get yourself wed. One of the stable boys, was it?" She already knew it wasn't, but she could always hope. She saw Martha straighten herself a little.

"I haven't told him yet. I will, then it will be well."

Oh Martha, I believe you are stupid, she thought. "Was it Able?" she asked, knowing it wasn't, but still clutching to the hope that it could have been one of her own.

Martha shrank back from Mrs Cook, perhaps worried she would be hit. "William." She whispered.

Mrs Cook closed her eyes. Like father like son. The second son of the Angehard family. "Oh my girl," she sighed. "You have no hope there. You need to be wed now, or deal with it. Do you understand?"

Martha looked aghast. "Mrs Cook, you can't suggest a murder. Why, did the reverend not say that was a witch's way?"

"Never mind the reverend's nonsense. This isn't a problem he'd ever have to deal with. We have to make our way in this world, and it is not a world that is kind to us women."

Martha brushed off her hands. "William will stand by me."

"He won't. They never do."

The young maid's lips pursed into a harsh thin line. "You best mind yourself, Mrs Cook, for when I am your lady..."

"Don't be ridiculous." She was a little taken aback by the sudden confidence. Martha was only fourteen, surely she couldn't be that deluded, that sure of herself. Everyone knew what happened to poor women when they fell with child out of wedlock, and none of them ever married the squire's son.

The two women turned sharply at a noise from inside the kitchen. Mary watched her rat nervously dart away through a tunnel through the chopped logs, then turned her eye to the crack in the door frame. They couldn't see any one, and no further noise nor voice was heard. Yet there was a tension in the air. Mrs Cook dropped her hands. "You know my thoughts. I'll help you if you wish..."

"That's the sort of talk the reverend said the dark..."

"Don't you dare threaten me."

Martha lowered her eyes.

"I'd think on it, if I were you. Don't do anything rash. I'll pray you see sense soon."

Sadly Martha did not see sense.

That night when the servants retired for bed, Martha twisted Mary's ear and pinched the skin on the underside of her arms, berating her for telling her secrets to Mrs Cook. She still wasn't sure how the dark haired girl had known, but she must have been spying on her. She'd be the first to go when Martha got to decide about things here.

It took a good two weeks for the bruises from Martha's pinches to go down. The nights weren't quite as cosy now Martha was in a mood and wouldn't let Abigail-Mary snuggle up with her. The two girls dropped off into exhausted, dreamless sleep in close isolation. Abigail fell quiet, felt the loneliness of her position and wished she could go back to her mother. She could become a lazy girl, get things wrong on purpose and maybe Mrs Cook would fire her and send her back to her mother. But she knew Mrs Cook would see through anything like that, and besides she had promised her grandmother that she would make it work. Because she needed to be here, although she didn't really understand why. She spoke little and got on with her chores, taking moments to go feed her pet rat crumbs in the woodshed when the opportunity arose.

When Mrs Cook was less harried, Abigail liked to stay in the kitchen. Mrs Cook would talk to the girl, teach her songs as they worked at the bread or plucked chickens. It was like being with her mother or her grandmother, not as nice of course, but there were tales to be learned. And Mrs Cook taught her new things. She was learning to make candles. Saved a fortune if they could make their own, Mrs Cook said.

She had sent Abigail-Mary down into Kilburn village to buy some string for the wicks. She had the package tucked safely away in her pocket, and had strode up the hill, past the carpenter's and the fresh scent of wood-curled shavings. A place of creation. She would linger if she could, for a minute or two, to try and see what the men were working on. Loitering near the doorpost, she had been watching one man with a file, before the chatter of children had distracted her, and she had looked around to see the Flintoff children scrabbling down the cart track road. They were a healthy, bubbling brood of contradictions. Most of the children were the average sort, who would make steady farmers and good wives, but nothing memorable. Intermingled were what some saw as curses, or as blessings, depending on who you asked. There was little Maisie, a year younger than Abigail, who was a stunning child, like something that had been sent down from heaven. Somehow she remained unblemished where other children carried scars of disease, malnutrition or squabbling. She was easily doted upon at this age, but women shook their heads knowingly. She'd grow to be a great beauty, a great distracting beauty, and that would cause trouble. Nothing good ever came of beauty.

Nothing good ever came of disfigurement either. One of Maisie's older brothers, Frederick, was nine and apprenticed to the carpenters. He had defied local opinion that he would soon waste away and die. They'd been saying it from the day he was born, with his misformed, shrunken right arm that was good for nothing. Lesser families would have declared a curse and looked around for the witch responsible. Perhaps if he had been born today some poor local woman would have been hurried away to the York assizes to explain herself. But the Flintoffs accepted life as it came, and his mother had been full of compassion. And Frederick thrived. He had inherited his father's easy, optimistic manner, and as he learned to walk and talk, he learned to do everything else one handed. His body knew no different. He would not be a cripple dependent on alms and begging, and had gone on to surprise his father when he had adapted his way to the working of wood, managing despite the use of only one hand. The local carpenter had not been interested at first when it had been suggested he could take Frederick on and teach him, but when he had seen the boy work, and taken in the lad's work ethic and dedication, he had found himself caught up in the enthusiasm. Despite everything, Frederick thrived. God clearly had a plan for him.

Abigail watched the cluster of children clatter on by, and missed her own siblings. Her own home, and fireside place. Her mother's hugs. Then she remembered herself and her errands, and started back to the hall. Hopefully she wouldn't be too late, and then Mrs Cook would still be in good humour and would teach her the art of candle making.

She entered the property by a side gate into the gardens, and hurried around to the back yard towards the kitchen Some of the pots the gardener used had been knocked over – thankfully not broken – and were lying in the path. Abigail paused to pick them up and leave the stack by a rose bush, assuming the gardener had left them out there for a reason.

"Don't leave clutter in Mamma's flower beds, you little peasant."

Abigail looked up, but neither moved nor straightened herself. Mrs Cook was still working on her manners towards her betters, and tended to keep Abigail-Mary out of sight from the Angehard family until she had developed a better sense of self preservation.

It was the youngest of the three sons, Henry, who had spoken. He was an awkward youth, suddenly shot up into gangling height and uncertain of what to do with his limbs. He was graced with intelligence but not with charm, and particularly feared interactions with women kind. He had not inherited the self-conceited, unquestionable confidence of his father. Such traits had naturally gone down to the eldest, Montague, who would eventually be the next squire of Kilburn. The second son, William, had been cast in the opposite direction and feared far too little the interactions with womenkind. He was a son that the family did not know what to do with, and would probably, with time be shipped off into a commission in the army. Henry would be going south to study eventually, for he was destined for the church.

Henry coloured. Children were just as incomprehensible as women to him. He was almost about to start stuttering, to turn and leave the vicinity, when he reminded himself of his status. Then he remembered that the child ought not to be staring so brazenly at him. Who did this dirty little housemaid think she was? "You ought to avert your stare and mind your manners," he hissed at her as if she were a naughty little sister.

"Avert your gaze?" Brother William laughed as he returned to the rose garden, glad to see those pots had been tidied up post drama. "Are you taking a walk out in the nip, brother? Avert your gaze ladies, for a fine specimen strolls by."

"There's no ladies here."

Abigail realised she shouldn't have stared. She dropped her eyes to the pots.

"You're not intimidated by this scruffy little maid? Why, she's just a child!"

"Of course I'm not. This child needs to learn some respect."

"You going to teach her?" William leered.

"Not all of us have such a fascination with the servants. Besides, I would have thought this one was too young even for you."

I need to leave, Abigail thought, picking up the pots and skirting around Henry. The brothers barely noticed her leave, background shadow that she was. Besides, in sibling rivalry, trading insults was enough to keep the boys entertained. She took the pots into the shed and left them by some sacking before running to the kitchen.

Mrs Cook was in good humour, for the bread had baked well and there was a sweet, malted scent in the kitchen. She heard Abigail-Mary come in, but didn't look up from her work. "Where have you been?"

"Got the string," Abigail took the package from her skirt pocket.

"Away with you then, let's get these candles started." Mrs Cook left the bread and walked to the pantry, knowing that Mary would be trotting behind her. She was glad of Mary's company today, something innocent and unbroken. She didn't want to be alone. She'd heard some of the arguing outside in the garden, and knew at some point the mistress would be down demanding Martha be expelled from the property and scolding Mrs Cook for not keeping a better eye on her staff. They were always "her" staff when something went wrong. Those wanton lying harlots. They were up to devilry with their tricks. Oh Martha, Mrs Cook sighed inwardly. I do not wish to have that conversation with you, so I will cower in the pantry with Mary and make candles, hoping the badness will all go away.

As things worked out, she didn't need to say anything to Martha, for the girl left on her own accord. Mrs Cook was informed the following morning, although the entire household already knew by then, in fact the entire village was talking of nothing else. Mrs Cook was instructed to hire a new girl immediately.

The following week when Mary was told to take a pail of water to Martha, she spent a great deal of time walking about the property with the heavy bucket, and in fact passed the woman twice before she realised that Jennifer Ruckle, who was clearing out the fireplace, was in fact Martha. Martha. As if nothing had happened or changed.

"Martha, I have the water."

Jennifer ignored her.

"Martha, I..."

Jennifer paused and looked up at Mary, before glancing about the hall and realising they were the only two people in the room. "You mean me, don't you? Sorry, my love. This will take some getting used to. Can't say I like taking a dead woman's name."

Mary's eyes widened as she passed across the bucket. "Who's dead?"

"Martha."

"Martha, you mean our Martha?"

"Well, I hardly mean myself, do I?" she scoffed. "I mean the girl before. Did you not hear? They found her drowned, out at the old mire." She paused in her scrubbing, and sitting up on her haunches, twisted to look at Mary full in the face. "Is it true that she was with child? That's why she committed the sin?"

"The sin?"

"Taking her own life." Jennifer considered Mary. "Are you simple in the head?"

"Don't think so."

"I heard some rumours that it might have been the master up here. Not that folk like to say such things too loudly, for I hear the squire would have anyone horsewhipped for speaking ill of his family. But do I need to watch out for him?"

"William."

"The son," Jennifer nodded. "Aye, I can see he's got a roving eye. A lass is best prepared."

"Will be you all right?"

Jennifer gave her a wink. "Don't you worry. This lass has a few ways to deal with lads with wandering hands."

Jennifer-Martha managed to avoid the men for the first two months, seeing her safely through late autumn and neatly into winter. She had the kind of ripeness about her body that clawed men's eyes away from what they were doing. Set against the backdrop of an old woman and a young, scrawny child, she seemed to be illuminated. She was canny at moving, at disappearing when William sensed his chance, or getting herself in with company so that none would dare jump her. In December the snows set in, and the family received fewer visitors, grew bored in their housebound state. Even the servants had less to do as they could not get out. The lads kept the firewood piles stocked, and the two maids spent regular trips about the house making certain the fires were kept blazing. The family would trip over Abigail-Mary as they would the dogs, but give her less consideration and certainly no scraps from their table. William stalked Jennifer and one evening as she was setting more logs on the fire in the dining hall, cold and empty despite the glow, he caught up with her.

Jennifer was not a weak lass. She had been working all her life, and came from a line of hearty country women who had been given their lot of minding house, beasts and children. She put up a fight, gave him as good as his gave, which would have ended the attempt for most men. But William, the second son who was never given anything for free and begrudged his elder for not dying of the fever when he was ten and holding on to the family property, would not be beaten by one of the peasants who ought to show deference for their betters. He punched her in the side of the head, the impact sending her face onto an awkward angle at the corner of the table and knocking two of her teeth out. The impact unbalanced her, sending sense skittering across the stone floor. It was all William needed to roll her over onto her front and hitch her skirts up.

As she lost the battle, Jennifer wanted to weep for letting such a weak minded man win over her. The teeth rattled in her mouth as he bashed away at her rear end. Her eyes rolled up in her skull and she caught sight of a fluttering figure darting from a crack in the door. Little Mary, who was too much the invisible child just yet. But she'd grow up and her time would come. She had given Mary to think that they could overcome. It wasn't the resigned fate of every maid to end up floating face down in the mire. She grinned to herself, blood rimmed teeth, and summoned her strength to clench and draw in, so hard till it closed. William's moans turned to sobs of agony. Then he hammered on her back to let him go.

The next day Jennifer merely hummed when Mrs Cook question her on the bruising and the swollen jaw. She took a cup of salt water, rinsing her mouth out and spitting out into the yard. Then, teeth jangling in her pocket, she fetched a small tankard of vinegar and the knobbled stalk end of the cabbage Mrs Cook had just soaked her bottom skirts in the snow to fetch. Jennifer wandered off to the woodshed, saying she was attending to a small problem, and that was that.

Upstairs William had taken to his bed, moaning and sweating in his sleep, screaming when he had to piss. A doctor was called, as much good as he was, and he attended the patient. The door was closed, muffling the howls, before there were mutterings on the top of the stairs between doctor and patron. The mother was kept out of discussions. The father, Squire Angehard, and his eldest, Montague, attended the afflicted, demanding to know what had happened. It took a week before William admitted to the source of his illness, with attempts to embellish who exactly was to blame for what. The squire knew protesting lies when he heard them, but when he saw how confidently, how healthily Martha went about her duties, he felt a fury that the natural order of things had been mocked. The wench wore a smug look on her face as if she held something over the family. He thundered at his son, for really this situation should never have happened. What kind of man let a woman do this to him? No squire's son ever let the peasantry get the better of them. It was off to the army for him once the winter had passed. He'd buy him a commission, but by god, the army would make a man of him where clearly the Squire had failed.

To redress the imbalance in social order that he perceived, he and his eldest son caught Martha alone in the very same room where all the trouble had started. Locking the doors, they beat and repeatedly raped the woman until they got her to hoarsely spit out that she was a witch whore of a bitch. She was then tossed into a small cell in the corner of the stables, rarely used but reserved for criminals that the squire occasionally had need of processing before they were moved on to York. The reverend from Coxwold, a man with a particularly devout reputation, was sent for. Abigail-Mary saw him arrive and set out his books and manuscripts upon the grand table. His trusted King James Bible. His crucifix. The treatises upon the nature of witches. Jennifer-Martha was interrogated. The squire informed his increasingly hysterical wife that the new maid had confessed to witchcraft. She was to watch the other two servants, lest they had been drawn into Satan's ways. Although he hoped they had caught the witch out in good time and the rest of the household would be safe now.

Villagers grew pale as word got around as it inevitably did. Many took the news at face value. Always thought those Ruckles had a way about them. Women, some at least, and some of the more reflective men, shared quiet knowing stares. It was common knowledge about the manor house's appetite for serving women, and someone was being taught a lesson. A lesson that the entire community would have sense to bide. Whatever people decided they believed, there was an unspoken common understanding that no one would be sending their daughters to work there again. The Angehards had to go to the hirings at Thirsk, or out up on the moors, to get their new staff from then on.

When Abigail-Mary stood at the crossroads outside the village, she'd note the looks people gave her, mostly pity, and catch comments whispered to one another when it felt safe to express a true opinion. Abigail looked back at the earthen mound, unmarked and already ignored. Come summer it would be covered in plants, buried under the undertow. Bramble creepers could come over and claim it back. Beneath the heap of dirt lay Martha and her unborn. Suicide was a sin and such a girl could not be buried in holy ground. What would she have thought about the fate of the next Martha? Was it better to resist, or to go with the flow and fool yourself that it was your own choice?

Grandmother appeared at the back door before the gloaming dawn of Abigail's monthly day off. The sudden appearance, coupled with a look in her eye made Abigail aware for the first time that people's pity wasn't just about the household she worked in. Grandmother and Mrs Cook were muttering in the open back doorway, eyebrows lowered with grave old-women expressions. Only nuances of their faces appeared, illuminated by the weak natural light, and the candle that Mrs Cook had set on a low cupboard just inside the door. She heard Abigail rustle out of her bench bed in the kitchen - she had been sleeping there for warmth since she was left alone in the servant bed in the attic - and looked pained.

"Grandmother?"

"Yes, it is I, lass. Come away now, before the village gets up."

"But I will have chores to do," Abigail-Mary said as she swung her legs over the side of the bench.

"Not today, Mary," Cook told her. "It's your day off." She turned back to the grandmother. "She'll be back here tomorrow morning?"

Grandmother nodded. Cook looked at her closely. "I won't be able to get you where I usually do now, will I?"

"Not anymore."

Cook looked to the ground. "These are dark times we are living in."

Grandmother pursed her lips. "We must pray for the light of the Lord," she said, although she didn't sound as though she meant it.

Abigail had quickly dressed, and appeared at Cook's side. "Are we going somewhere?"

"Come away now, oh child," Grandmother said, taking her by the hand and leading her out of the back paths, ways of servants and the labouring classes. They would escape from the manor house, if only for a day. They walked quickly through the village, Abigail's fingers slipping back into their place around Grandmother's worn grasp. They walked past a cabin cart, something that looked like a container to transport livestock that would overwise leap out of the top and away. There was a dank scent of misery about it, although it currently stood empty. It had only been here overnight until it would be away in the morning proper to other villages close by.

Grandmother paled when she saw it, and lowered her head, muttering, "My God."

Abigail paused for a moment to stare before she was tugged away by her grandmother's eager pace. "Will they be taking Martha away in that?"

"Martha?"

"Jennifer Ruckle. The maid. They have her locked up and say she is a witch but I don't believe it." She faltered when she saw grandmother's expression. "Or should I believe it?" she asked uncertainly, fearful she'd said something wrong. She was careful not to speak much or have any thought or opinion in the manor house, but with grandmother she'd always been encouraged to ask and learn.

"Not the witches they speak of, no," Grandmother shook her head and continued walking. They headed uphill, out of the village and into the forests, where she felt safer to speak. "The nonsense the men speak of does not exist. It's just an excuse to cover over petty revenge and hate. That and a twisted lust," she added quietly to herself.

"Mrs Cook said they're going to take Martha to the York assizes. I don't know what that is."

"It is the courthouse. Folk can accuse, but the court will decide what's right and wrong. Who is guilty, and who is innocent. Punish those who they think need to be punished."

"So if there's no such thing as witches, they'll send Martha home."

Grandmother smiled sadly, "Justice doesn't work that way. Not for women like us. Now, we shall away to Osmotherley today, over the hills to the far distance like you always wanted to."

Abigail burst out into an innocent grin. "Really?"

"Really," Grandmother nodded to her. "And you shall learn the way, so you can always find your way back. Let's start at the beginning. Get us up to the top of the cliffs and the gallops and we'll take it from there."

It was the early part of the year and the forest was dripping and muddy, crusts of ice broken open to reveal chilly water and sloppy mud below. The naked trees, twisted arms and fingers, curled up towards a grey sky. The air was saturated with damp: a healthy, living forest layer that settled in the lungs as they breathed it in, puffing their way up the steep bank. Grandmother said it was a long walk to Osmotherley, and the light would not be on their side, so they must be swift and they would be walking most of the day. At the top of the slopes the moors abruptly stopped for the break of cliffs and vistas down over the Vale of Mowbray. They walked even faster. Despite the biting wind and low temperatures, Abigail's breath puffing and condensing around her, she worked up a sweat as they moved over the bleak landscape. Here was always the last place spring would touch. They passed by farmland and forestry, before coming out onto the moorland of Snilesworth. In the height of summer this landscape that touched the endless horizon would be a blazing purple, the air heavy with the scent of the tiny shrub flowers. Now the heather was a mass of rough-brown, scratchy hands that tugged at skirts as the two walked by. Abigail was an energetic little girl used to work, used to being on her feet, and yet this walk was trying on her legs. She ached, she longed to stop, but Grandmother wouldn't even pause to take something to eat. It was only when they were far out on the moors, following a dirt trackway that Grandmother told her was the drover's road, that she abruptly stopped.

"You go straight on there on this road, and you'll get to the Chequers farm. It's a stop off for the drovers from Scotland."

"They walk as far as we do?"

Grandmother smiled gently. "Much further. They walk from Scotland to London. It takes weeks. And there," she continued, shifting her arm easterly. "That is Black Hambleton, that hill. Mind the name and remember it. It is a landmark to keep you true. Keep it to your right. There are hidden caves in there should you need the shelter."

"If it is raining?"

The old woman stared keenly at the young girl. "Any kind of shelter. The land will know to care for you, for you are one of the folk."

Abigail didn't listen to the undertones, but somewhere in her subconscious the understanding was laid down. Years from now she would recall this moment with disturbing clarity.

"And Osmotherley?"

Her arm swung to the west. "Before you get to Chequers, there is a path that goes down the gully bank. After the hill. That will take you to the village. We head for Chequers this day. But first we need to go somewhere."

They circumnavigated the bleak, foreboding height of Black Hambleton, and headed deeper into the moors, leaving the drover's road far behind, abandoning even the paths the locals took. They followed what looked like a meandering sheep rut. Abigail kept close to her grandmother, for she was not sure she would ever find her way back to the world from here. At last they reached a slight mound, where twelve wind-battered rocks protruded from the heather at all angles to form a loose circle. They entered the circle, the wind blowing their hair out of their bonnets and whipping it across their faces; their skirts billowing heavily to the side. Then the wind dropped and the atmosphere calmed. Grandmother sat down in a bed of heather, and Abigail copied her, pleasantly surprised to find the heather strong and springy enough to keep her well off the wet ground.

"This is a place of sanctuary, and we are here to talk," Grandmother said. "But first we must eat."

Abigail caught the little bag of food that was thrown to her. She stretched out her legs, the soles of her feet blissfully grateful to be relieved of load bearing pressure. She tore into the bread, her hunger waking as she felt the food in her hands. For some time neither person communicated, focused on eating.

After some time, the old woman raised her head and regarded her granddaughter. "We can speak freely here," she said. "When we go back, we must guard our tongues again. There is a sickness upon this land, upon the minds of men. They have placed themselves in positions of power, and to make their thrones higher, they tell us we are foolish and stupid. Easily led by evil. And yet fully culpable for all we do, real or not."

Abigail placed the bag on her lap, not really sure what Grandmother was talking about.

"You know that a woman's place is in silent servitude. She must not be seen or known to have an opinion. And if others seek her advice, it unsettles our leaders. They fear they will be usurped. These are dark, dangerous times, Abigail. We must be so careful."

Silence fell down around them. Abigail was still not entirely sure what her grandmother was trying to tell her. She realised with a sense of horror that the old woman was sobbing. She felt a dread in the pit of her stomach. She did not think she wanted an explanation, for once known, it could not be undone. She would soon be eight years old. This felt too heavy a thing. "Grandmother?"

She wiped her face with her hands. Drew in her breath. There were things that needed to be said, and they needed to be at Chequers before nightfall. "You have heard of the witches. That which the reverend speaks of in church. It is all distorted lies."

Abigail's eyes widened. "The church is lying?"

Grandmother held up her hand. "Remember, we do not speak of these things outside of the circle. You saw the cart that will take

Jennifer Ruckle away to York, for she has been accused of witchcraft. Some women are released, for the accusations are so ridiculous no man in his right mind could follow through. But the King bays for blood, and some have too much influence to let such women live. You understand what I say? If a woman is found guilty, she will be killed."

"Jennifer will..."

"I'm not sure how her case will go. Although she has embarrassed the Angehards, which will not tell in her favour. Abigail, they are having a purge in our villages. There are a lot more than just Jennifer who are being transported to York." She pressed her lips together, feeling her eyes watering. "My poor daughter."

"I'm all right," Abigail scuttled across to the old woman's side. "I'm here."

She ran a hand over the top of the girl's head. "I know, but I grieve for my daughter."

Abigail sometimes forgot that people had lives and connections outside of herself. It was hard to imagine Grandmother as a young woman, or that she'd ever had daughters of her own.

"The gossip will spread today, and when you go back tomorrow, everyone will be talking of it. I needed to tell you before you heard another way. So you know the truth. And so that you are prepared. For you must not react, you must keep your head down and be about your work. Don't draw attention to yourself.

"Grandmother." Abigail nestled into the woman's side and closed her eyes. She didn't want to know anymore.

"My dear girl, your dear mother has been accused," Grandmother wept. "They pinched her skin and made her bleed. They have said terrible things. She will be taken to York. They will not let her come home. My poor darling Kerenza. Your heart was too kind and you helped too many."

"Mamma?" Abigail balled up fistfuls of shawl within her fingers, feeling a panic rise in her gut. "You don't mean they will kill my Mamma?"

"You must be strong. You must stay quiet. We must not be noticed."

Abigail started to wail. She darted up, as if she would run to her mother, but grandmother's arm shot out and held her fast. "There is nothing we can do," she said as the girl sobbed into her side. "I'm so sorry my girl. This life is hard enough without the evils of men. She is taken now, and gone from us. You must mourn her here so that we can stay in the shadows out there. Oh little one," she sighed, stroking the girl's back. "We are so terribly alone in this world."

There was a thump on her back.

It gave her pause.

Abigail half turned, expecting to see someone there, but she was quite alone on the track. There was a jeer, and she saw the little cluster of children by the dead bracken, fistfuls of wet earth at the ready. A couple more projectiles were lobbed, one missing her by several feet, the other hitting her on the thigh. It left a brown smear on her dress. The soil clung for a moment before dropping inertly to the ground.

"Witch's child!"

"Devil spawn!"

Abigail started crying, the word Mamma whispered in her mouth. Her own dear Mamma who only ever tried to help people. Children with fevers, women in the birthing bed. Men who needed bones setting. That she was tired from tending her own family and home never stopped her going to people's aid when they called for her. How could anyone wish her ill?

It was only the day after grandmother had told her of what was coming. Abigail was walking back to Kilburn on her own. They had walked to Chequers farm, on the high moors above Osmotherley, and spent the night there. Grandmother knew the farmer's wife of old, and had gone there to live and work. She would never return to her home, to her village or her own land. It was too dangerous there now, better than they were split up and quiet, hidden. They both needed to mind their counsel, stay inside and keep busy with their work. Wait until all of this had died down and people had moved on to the next drama. They must hold on to their tears until the deepest moments of night. There was nothing they could do to help her mother. No even praying, Grandmother had said, when Abigail had asked. The God that oversaw this would never listen to a woman's pleas. The devil had played the greatest trick, and fooled the men in power that he spoke the word of God. He told them to torture and kill innocent people, and they said lo, it is the word of the Almighty, and Satan laughed. God looked to the side and let it happen.

Abigail had cried relentlessly as she walked alone along the drover's road over the high moors. Through the biting wind, away from the warm glow of Chequers. She was a speck in the wilderness, moving past Black Hambleton Hill, and away to the seemingly endless moorland plateau of browned-off heather that was always the last of the plants to show life in the year. She sobbed for her Mamma. For thinking that the hug she had received just before she had gone away to work at Kilburn, had actually been the last hug she ever would have. She hadn't known it at the time, and she wanted to go back, linger over the intimacy, and tell her Mamma everything. She wanted to hear that her Mamma loved her. And maybe she could have taken her Mamma away with her. Or warned her, or done something, so that today might never have needed to pass. Home would not be home anymore, even if Pa and her brothers and sisters stayed. And Grandmother had left her home. There was nowhere to run to, no little safe sanctuary to hide in. She might hide under her blanket on the bed, except it would be cold and lonely there now that Jennifer-Martha had gone. Or maybe she should stay in the little kitchen bench bed she sometimes slept on when she was too tired to drag herself upstairs to the servants' quarter.

A clod of earth to the side of the face woke her up to the present moment. The children laughed and congratulated one another at a good aim. Abigail started to run, hurrying further down the path and out of reach of their projectiles. It took longer to get away from the sound of their laughter. As if a child losing their mother was funny.

It had rained last night, and the ground was wet, the mud loose and sloppy. A jump over a gnarled, creeping tree root saw her footing unsure when she landed, and she slipped. Her feet flew out and she bounced on her bottom downwards a little way before laying back in the filthy mud and feeling the wind escape her lungs. She felt the wet earth press itself around her, gum her hair and stain her skirts. Mrs Cook would be furious when she returned to the hall covered in mud. Could she just skip out on life instead? Stay in the forest and live in the trees? She gazed up at the mesh of tree branches, seemingly bare, with only the tight bud knobbles of the promise of leaves and spring if one knew where to look. The trees would be a peaceful place to be. There wasn't anywhere Abigail really wanted to go.

A face appeared above her in the middle air between the wet ground and the woodland canopy. A concerned crease, that evened out when it showed that Abigail was neither dead nor unconscious. Frederick Flintoff from the village. Had he been throwing stones and mud at her?

"Abigail Craister," he said, and for the first time Abigail wondered that he would know who she was. He ought not to be in favour in the village, for a child with a deformed, useless arm would have been viewed by many as a waste of food and effort. Yet he proved his worth and was said to be doing well in his apprenticeship. And he had such pretty siblings, the glow of which had probably saved him.

"You ought to get up and get back to the hall," he told her, offering his good hand to pull her to her feet. Abigail accepted his hand as she realised none of the Flintoff children had been in that little mob up the hill. She struggled to her feet, almost slipping over and grabbing hold of his forearm to balance herself.

"I am sorry to hear about your Ma," Frederick said.

Abigail opened her mouth in a ma-rounded shape, but found she couldn't make a sound. If she tried any harder, she knew her voice would wobble and she would start crying. He was right, she did need to get back to the hall. To disappear within its walls.

"They were talking about it at church today."

Church, she realised. It was the Sabbath, and she'd spent the morning walking back across the moors, crying and cursing a God that would do such a thing to her Mamma. She hadn't even thought of church, even though she had always diligently attended every Sunday.

"I can't believe all the horrible things they say. Pa says we should keep out of it."

The two children were the same height although Frederick was two years older. They stood in sombre silence, mud splattered boots, Abigail with muck plastered down the length of her back. Their eyes dropped, moving to Frederick's withered arm.

"Folk say I was cursed, that this..." he moved it. It was still a limb, still had movement to it. It was still him, even though some looked at it and said it was freakish. "I don't think there's much rhyme nor reason to most things," he said. "Things just happen. That's all."

"Bad things happen," Abigail whispered.

"Aye, that they do."

The two children started down the forest track towards the village of Kilburn. Frederick back to his family home, Abigail to the angry stare of Mrs Cook, who declared she was late back and who did she think she was taking much longer than her allotted time off. She walked around the girl, shaking her head in horror as she saw all the filth, both on her clothes and her face. She had asked where she had been, and Abigail had almost told her Osmotherley, before changing her response to 'away'. An unspoken sense that the fewer times it as spoken, the better for Grandmother. Mrs Cook had nodded, muttered that she had heard she had gone. And the muck? She had fallen over. Fallen over and rolled? Abigail had started to cry, and Mrs Cook relented. The girl would have been told. More unnecessary suffering in the world. She'd washed down the girl and put her to bed early, before scrubbing out her clothes and setting them to dry by the kitchen fire. They'd write today off, and be back to it tomorrow morning. Hopefully hard work and chores would keep her mind from losing almost everything dear to her in the world.

ADOLESCENCE

Eight Years Later
Yorkshire
Northern England

The Squire Montague Angehard, son of the late Squire Percival Angehard, stood at the first floor window and stared out upon his grounds with a hard look of the proprietor in his eye. His father had only been dead these three years past, and many still said how much better things had become with the inherited handover. To the son they would even ascribe things the old squire had actually completed; memories being short as to how swiftly time past.

His middle brother, William, had been shipped off to the army after that period of witch purging from the local villages. William thrived in his bought commission, did no real battle work or fieldcraft, but rose through the ranks, ordering the deaths of others in the name of the glory and the king, and fathering unwanted and unacknowledged bastards wherever he travelled. With all the drinking and eating and general inactivity, he had grown quite portly and red faced over the years. Loud and intensely boring, tolerated by many, but as far as Montague could ascertain, liked by none. He personally held optimistic and realistic hopes that his brother would be dead in the next few years.

His youngest brother was not quite so easy to dispose of. Sullen, but lean and healthy, and with a frustrating constitution that neither chill nor damp ever brought about illness, Henry had completed his studies in Oxford and been ordained in the church. Their father had arranged a living for him in a parish away in Norfolk – father had never taken to Henry either – but after a year, well-timed with father's death, Henry announced that he had better and more godly things to attend. He had departed from Norfolk and returned north to Yorkshire, where he currently resided, barely tolerated in the family home. At first he said that he had been called (never explaining who by) to rid these tracts of witches. The country was caught up in ridding itself of witches. Montague felt confident, most of the time, that they had been exceptionally swift and rid themselves of the disease early in the period. They had caught and sent off a number of women to the York assizes, most of whom had been found guilty and executed. Their quick, harsh action had sent a message through the community. The local women had been reminded of their place. There had been little trouble for some years.

With no obvious wickedness to disapprove of, Henry had turned inward and declared he wished a sole audience with God. He was to become something of a hermit. Probably because there was nothing else he was capable of doing. Montague had heard reports of his time in Norfolk and they were not complimentary. He seemed to have an inability to deal with people, either to listen and minster to them, or to command them. Women in particular were a problem, and Montague had been a little embarrassed to see Henry's behaviour when in the presence of a pretty face, even one that knew well enough to keep its eyes to the floor. It was a mixture of flushing angst, a look of coming nausea, and a trembling control not to lick the woman's feet. How was it that three men could have the same parentage and upbringing, and yet only one manage to grow to a decent example of manhood? Perhaps they did not credit the influence of witches with enough damage. For it had been William that the maid-witch had cursed, and Henry had been young at the time. An easily disturbed mind.

When Henry declared he was going to be a pious hermit, Montague did not much mind. Even when Henry decided to commandeer a small tract of family land, technically Montague's property and nothing to do with Henry, for his hermitage. It was a poor piece of land, up on the hills and rough uncultivated moorland. Any idiot living alone up there would soon perish after a few winters. And it was as far from the family home as one could get whilst remaining on their land, so the hope was with time, Montague could perhaps forget for the most part that he had any brothers.

Henry was busy with the construction this spring which kept him absent from the house frequently. Not that Henry did much, he was not practical in nature. Oddly he had brought in carpenters and stonemasons from down south, choosing to snub the local workforce, whom Montague was sure would have gladly done the work for at least half the price, happily serving their masters. Even in this error of judgement he indulged his brother if it meant it kept him out of the way.

Montague's reflective moment on the curve of the grand old staircase was paused as he noted through the diamonds of glass, a figure walking through the gardens. A young woman, whom he was assured had been working in his household for years, although he could only remembering noticing her for the last six months. Their housemaid Mary, blossoming and quite lovely. Generally pious in her apron and white cap, but he'd caught sight of those great long chestnut waves of hair. The slender wrist. Perhaps it was a mere distraction, for his wife, Isobella, was pregnant again and he was strictly leaving her alone this time in the hopes she might finally produce a son and heir. They had two girls whom Isobella doted on, but Montague found them rather insipid, with those pleading eyes they had inherited from the other side of the family. He'd say it was womanly witchery, only he saw his father-in-law in those eyes. A strange man, far richer and prosperous than the Angehards and yet a man unaware of his place in society. He had an unnatural understanding with his staff and tenants, a poor sense of judgement in letting them tell him what he ought to do. The man was lucky he had not been robbed blind and left destitute. Some of Montague's own staff had gotten ideas above their station having watched this man on visits to their home. Isobella, damaged by her upbringing, had shown too much sympathy to that old housemaid of theirs, Martha. Actually coming to her husband and taking the housemaid's part in the drama. A drama brought on by the girl's witchery. A man in charge of his own mind would never touch such a girl, any fool could see that. She had been explicit in the look in her eyes and the movement of her hands. Had she not wished it so, a cunning she-devil like her would have acted appropriately. Isobella was weak minded, worse for being a woman, and she had been with child at the time. Easily manipulated. She had forgotten the commandment: honour and obey thy husband. Demanded he stop. He had taught her a lesson, and yes, it had been unfortunate that she had lost the baby shortly after, but it had been collateral damage. The wife was better behaved and obedient now and the household would run more smoothly, according to his needs.

Mary-Abigail paused by the turned over vegetable plots and felt that she was being watched. She turned to look up at the house and saw a shadow shift from the staircase window. This sense of being watched, of ill will, had been growing upon her in recent months. Mrs Cook had been increasingly particular about widening her mop caps and making sure every strand of her hair was hidden. Of providing misshapen aprons that would reduce her figure to a lump, never that successfully, and taking Mary- Abigail's chin between two fingers to examine her face, and with a sigh wish that she didn't look so much like her mother.

No matter. Picking up her basket, she skipped like the child she no longer was, moving along the gravelled paths and out of the walled garden to the track to the village. Abigail was sixteen and increasingly aware that the locals viewed her differently. Not only an adult, but an adult female, which put her into a class similar to cattle as far the assessing eyes of men were concerned. She had been a late developer, and busy with her work in the hall, she wasn't seen as frequently as other local girls. There were plenty her age who were already betrothed or married and expecting children. Abigail would glance at those girls from the side, at their blossoming stomachs, and wonder if one felt ready for such things at some point. If something clicked in the mind and one knew one was a woman. Ready for those things in life. She'd tried to ask her Grandmother about it once, but Grandmother said she was best staying out of the sight of men for now. The past few years had not been kind to the common woman. Grandmother had shrank into herself, both literally in age and in society. She did not trust men, to the point she positively hated them, with their superior position in society and their preaching. Their talk of devilry and witches. Abigail wondered how she had ever managed to have her own children, for she knew a man was required in the begetting of babes.

Instinctively she darted up to the side of the road when she saw Henry Angehard in the village. He stood close to the village inn, flicking through paper in his hands. He had probably come down from his moorland retreat to collect his post. He was a sallow-eyed, skittish thing. If he had been a creature, Abigail would have believed he had been ill-used in his youth, beaten by his master and nervous of what was right. Yet he had been raised in comfort with privilege, and the look of guilt of things not even yet committed didn't sit right with the Angehard family crest. His eyes started to rove across the villagers milling about before the inn, and Abigail unconsciously pushed herself up against the front garden wall of a cottage. Apple blossom drifted down to settle on her cap and shoulders. Every cottage had its own garden, and was cunningly packed with fruit trees, vegetables and herbs. Families had to grow all they could to sustain themselves, and in spring the village was a delight of tree blossom, going through the apples, pears, plums and gauges. When the sun shone on the yellow sandstone built cottages, the lush foliage of the orchards, all to the soundtrack of happy bees, chickens clucking about their runs and people chattering, it was a joyful, alive place to be. More so than in the brooding, watchful passageways of the hall.

"Why, Abigail Craister, I'm sure that wall won't be falling down soon," a gentle voice tinkled. The perfect face to the sunlight moment of village idyl brushed past Abigail. There went Maisie Flintoff, a year junior to Abigail, and at fifteen, somehow miraculously unmarked by either illness or parasite. She was a beauty. She was still without a sweetheart, and many a family would have cursed having yet another daughter to have to marry off. Maisie was so beautiful, and well mannered and kind to go with it, that men would probably pay the Flintoffs a dowry themselves if it meant they could take Maisie home. Abigail smiled awkwardly at Maisie. She was always kind, and the gentle teasing was never meant as anything more, yet Abigail always felt her curious angles and outsider status more when set beside Maisie. It had been long since she had been part of the brood of children of her own kin, and she had not been pretty enough for local lads to lust after.

She drew her eyes away from Maisie as she passed, then without thought looked back up at the inn boldly and directly at Henry Angehard. The man was watching Maisie intently, and the pallor of his skin had turned rather sickly. The man was almost visibly trembling. Maisie was so far beneath him in status, he ought not to be affected at all. Lords and common girls only led to one thing, Mrs Cook would constantly remind her, and she had seen that time and again with the Marthas. Better not to be seen and relegated to the background. Perhaps Abigail was lucky. Maisie attracted too much attention. It was not her fault, she certainly didn't attempt it with flirting or ungodly dress. But if a man was disgruntled, it soon became the woman's blame.

She hurried down the road, keeping her eyes down and her body lost to the bustle, slipping past a chain of donkeys and keeping them between Henry Angehard, his men and herself. He didn't notice her, for his attention was still on the retreating figure of Maisie Flintoff. Abigail rounded the corner down a side track and almost tumbled into an approaching wheelbarrow. She backed up, skirts twisting around her, and caught her breath in a gasp. The man dofted his cap to her, necessitating setting down the barrow for he only had one good arm. "Good Morrow to you, Miss Craister."

Abigail broke out into a grin, hearing Mrs Cook's voice somewhere in her subconscious that she ought not to be so openly friendly and pleasant to a man. But Frederick Flintoff had always been very kind to her, even when they had been children. She lifted her basket, unable to take the grin off her face. "Away on my errands," she told him.

"Aye, Miss Craister," he nodded. "That's what we're all about just now."

Later that day, when she had finished her chores and found herself in a pause before the main dinner preparations, Abigail would smile to herself as she hummed and thought about Frederick Flintoff again. She was crouched down in her usual hiding place in the woodshed, feeding her pet rats crumbs. Mrs Cook would have a fit if she knew Abigail was actively encouraging rodents. But these three were canny and well behaved, and knew how to keep out of the kitchen cat's way, unlike many of their other cousins. They were very trusting of Abigail, and would happily sit upon her knee and allow her to stroke them between the ears. She could tell them apart from the other rats on the property. The nests that the head gardener was always destroying in the manure heaps. The ones that would never leave the cabbages alone. So bold with the desperation of survival, they did not always think. But these three were more canny. They had caught on to the game, and knew when to wait and observe. They knew when and where to hide, to wait for opportunity. And they were affectionate company for Abigail, telling her what she imagined was the news of the manor, the things they saw and heard and the comings and goings of the village. They were her closest friends, Grandmother and Mrs Cook aside. The Marthas were always hard to befriend. No sooner had she come to trust one, then the usual would happen, the girl disposed of and a new Martha in her place. It took so long to learn how much one could trust a person, that it didn't seem worth the effort to grow close to Martha these days. But the rats were loyal, and the rats stayed undercover. And she knew that if she had to ever call on them, they would have done anything for her.

That Sunday, the villagers and local farmers from the surrounding tracts filed into the church in a dour line of obedience and humility. The village church of St Mary's was a stocky Norman stone building, the blocks of masonry centuries carved and hallowed. It wasn't as grand as some of the other churches in the tract. Abigail had overheard her masters complain of the matter now and then, stating that there ought to be a bell tower. Nothing more had happened than talk. A tower would take a lot of money and perhaps their sins or desperation were not yet steep enough to warrant it.

The Angehard family had their own chapel at the manor house, which the staff were sometimes allowed to attend. Mrs Cook would use it in the winter, but in warmer months preferred the walk to the village. In the most recent year she had actively encouraged Abigail-Mary to go out to St Mary's. It gave Mrs Cook a brief period of contentment when she need not worry about that which she could not see.

Day to day Abigail-Mary did not get much rest from her duties, but the weekly attendance at church gave her respite, despite the cold hard pews. The villagers were so tightly packed inside, that it was impossible for one to fall over in sleep. There were plenty who had perfected the art of a devout appearance whilst actually resting or even sleeping. A chance to just be still and empty the mind was a blessing. Afterwards she would not rush back to work, but amble with the older Flintoff children, who seemed to have adopted her for this purpose – Frederick, Maisie and a couple of others. They would chatter and walk through the woodland, stopping by a small gushing stream to drink and splash each other. There was laughter and lighthearted joking. Abigail always felt awkwardly placed, not quite in the role she was meant for, but appreciated the kind gesture, and enjoyed those fleeting senses of being part of a family. She never saw her own kin, not since mother had been killed. The brood of children had been so great that father had effectively been forced to take on a new wife. The new woman was a decent enough sort, but listened to gossip too readily and watched Kerenza's offspring with suspicion. As soon as was decent they were sent out into service or apprenticeship, and she swiftly refilled the house with her own, more trusthworthy children. Abigail's siblings were scattered across the tract, and for the girls especially there was an unspoken understanding that they were better off keeping their heads down and not gathering. Already one had been lost, an older brother apprenticed to a blacksmith. A horse had kicked out during a shoeing, and the boy's head had momentarily been in an unfortunate position. They said he had been killed outright, and probably best for him, given his parentage. Some bitter old folks said the horse had sensed the beast in the boy. Her two older sisters were already wed with children of their own, too busy to remember their strange little sister who had been sent away to service far earlier than any other sibling. Almost as if mother had wanted rid of her. Best to steer clear of that one.

Gradually the Flintoff grouping started to break into factions on Sundays; the younger children who wanted to play, and the elders who preferred to amble and gossip, or had other places to be. Maisie would slip off on a side path with a coy smile on her lips, one of the sisters giggling about a new sweetheart. Soon Abigail found she was walking alone with Frederick. Decorum said she ought not to, but no one saw them, she had no family to remind her of better behaviour. What Mrs Cook didn't see she couldn't grieve over. More important than all of that was the simple fact that Abigail enjoyed their walks, to the point it was all that she could think of during the working week. On Saturday nights she struggled to fall asleep in anticipation.

On week Frederick did not come to church, for he was away at Thirsk with his employer on a commission and they would attend church in the market town that week. Abigail had felt so sorrowful that she couldn't even stomach hours with the rest of the Flintoff family, and had sneaked off through the woodland, easily disguising her retreat with the foliage, to sit alone in a little dell and weep a little. Her rats had found her, and lined up in the curve of her skirt, concerned and squeaking until they had got her to calm down. More people were getting betrothed in the village and she had even heard a couple of the old mothers joking that perhaps even Frederick Flintoff with his creepy arm might find himself a wife amongst the dairy maids. Dairy maids, Abigail thought huffily. As if he could do no better.

She couldn't stop smiling in church when she saw he was back at Kilburn, then felt ridiculous and embarrassed when she left the House of God, concerned everyone knew where her new serenity sprung from. She worried they knew Abigail Craister had ideas above her station, for Frederick Flintoff would soon be betrothed to a dairy maid.

The only thing to be done was to act normal, as if nothing had happened. As if dairy maids were no bother to her. She had joined the Flintoffs after church as usual but had lost the power of speech, had nothing of good sense to say. She followed her peers, swamped in horror of how feeble in mind she had become. She was readying herself to slip away, tired of watching Maisie chatter with her brother, arms linked together, when Maisie turned and looked Abigail directly in the eye.

"I'll be away now," she said, for the first time openly admitting that she liked to depart to secret rendezvous. "You'll keep my brother company, won't you, Abigail?"

And in a moment, she found herself alone in the forest with Frederick, wishing she could throw herself at him, but knowing she ought to walk away.

"Are you well, Abigail?" Frederick asked, touching her shoulder. "You're looking right wan."

Abigail felt as though she was in boiling laundry suds. "I am feeling feverish…" she started, hoping she could make her excuses and leave.

"Aye, there's a strange fever about. I've been away near enough a fortnight and I come home to all kinds of stories. Mother tells me I'm about to be married to a dairy maid…"

And there it was. Abigail felt the bottom of her chest drop out. She couldn't even look at him. She simply wanted to fold in on herself and disappear. "I wish you both the best of luck," she mumbled at the ground.

"Of course, I don't know what dairy maid this is supposed to be," Frederick continued, his voice pattern racing a little now. "I was always told not to expect anything like that in life, on account of this…" He couldn't find the word and they both looked to his misformed little arm, kept safe in special sleeves his mother stitched to his shirts. "Well, they always said I wouldn't even live long enough to be of an age for ought like that. And time has gone on and it seems I am of such an age now, and soon to finish my apprenticeship…"

They grew silent, the pair of them now awkwardly examining the earth track beneath their feet.

"When I was over in Thirsk," Frederick started up, embarrassed to feel a tremor darting at the edge of his voice. This was not the manly, persuasive speech he had planned over recent weeks. "Well, that is to say I did miss church. I mean after church. Our walks..."

Abigail dared to raise her eyes to his shirt.

"I mean to say, I did think about you whilst I was away." He did not feel this was going well, for she still kept her eyes away from him. She most certainly knew what he was about now, and would be embarrassed, for she would not want to take a cripple. Abigail was a kind lass, and would not want to hurt his feelings either. He was putting her into a terrible position. He ought to back off now and let her be, but now he had started, he felt he had to see it through to its miserable end if only to be able to say to himself that he had tried. "I don't suppose it would be possible, with me being a cripple, that you could think of me that way."

She braced her legs, feeling her knees about to buckle. Her heart was racing. She must have misheard, or misunderstood, yet here it was. She was struck dumb for a moment or two, staring at his shirt and feeling so giddy that she knew she would have to get away before she collapsed.

"I am sorry to have offended you, Miss Craister."

Miss Craister indeed. What rot, Abigail thought. "I have to go now," was what she managed to whisper.

Frederick felt his heart crack. Be strong, lad. You knew this was possible.

Her impulses pushed her awkward terror to the side for a moment, and she abruptly darted up to him, kissing him on the cheek and holding her face very close to his. "I missed you something awful too, Frederick Flintoff," she whispered. "I'll be looking forward to next Sunday."

She felt a hot hand on her arm, the heat coming through the cloth. The tension was a moment before the thunderstorm. He moved his head slightly, meeting her eyes with a bright sparkle. He kissed her on the mouth, before Abigail pulled away playfully. "Until next Sunday," she told him, darting up the woodland path before he had chance to pull her back.

Expectation and anticipation coloured the summer days in glorious hues. Chores and hard work at the manor seemed a blessing, for it made the time move faster and then it was Sunday or another late evening when they would get chance to sneak off into the woods to be together. If Mrs Cook suspected anything, she never made mention of it. Between worrying over the current Martha, and a leg infection of her own that was making walking difficult, Abigail-Mary was an afterthought to the background she did not notice. Grandmother, away in Osmotherley, assumed Abigail was either busy or unable to get away which was why she did not visit for months. She was keeping safe. Despite Abigail's joy and lightened step, these were still insecure times. Grandmother worried that it had been so long since her daughter's murder that the narrowminded and insecure grew bored and were starting to scratch around for new victims to blame their woes and deficiencies on.

Abigail was oblivious. Frederick said they were going to be married. His apprenticeship was done, he was saving money and soon it would be possible. Abigail would have been happy to leave the manor and live in abject poverty with him tomorrow, but he said it would be prudent to wait until the next hirings. Better to leave with the years pay and a good name. It wouldn't be all that long. Abigail had stopped sending her money home – it had ceased being a home to her a long time ago – and had a little purse hidden away in her rats' nest, guarded by her friends. Frederick still referred to her home, the place where her mother once lived, as her home, and said he would go to speak to her father soon. She didn't see the point, it was her choice who she wed and she hadn't heard from her father for years, but Frederick was keen on doing most things correctly. He wanted their married life to start right.

Most things at least. Although as they were both certain they would be wed before the year was out, youthful exuberance broke any notions of abstinence and they were soon man and wife in all but the notation in the parish records. Fingers stretched out through forest plants, old bluebell leaves, leaf litter and earth. Hair loose and splayed on the ground, the dappled sunlight setting off a glow in the waves. Abigail experienced the ripple of pleasure that would grow and move up through her inner self as she learned what men and women could do when left together in solitude. It was not what she had imagined, when watching the Marthas dry their eyes, clean themselves down afterwards. The wan, miserable expression during the grunting and thrusting by the lord and master. This was something different. It was consuming, both physically and mentally. She didn't notice the knowing looks from some of the local girls. Suddenly jealous that the odd witch's child had caught the freakish lad. That strange boy with the wizened arm, as if caught by a witch's spell in birth. Always positive and happy regardless, and he had grown to develop into quite a man regardless. Perhaps always prepared for his witch bride by the spell, so that no good, wholesome lass might chance to catch him.

Comments and observations, community judgements passed Abigail by. Maisie Flintoff, also filled with youth's summer love, couldn't help but see the looks between Abigail and Frederick. She'd sometimes drop hints to Abigail when they were walking together, but the girl never caught on. It was as if she'd missed some induction into the chatter of women, working from such a young age, and always on her own. She was a little odd, but a good soul, Maisie thought, and very canny at getting them away out of sight when the eyes of men grew too much. Maisie didn't like to talk about it, worried people would think her getting ideas above her station, but whenever they saw the squire's youngest son, she felt she could not move without him staring at her, mentally devouring her. She was relieved when his hermitage was completed. It was on a remote plain of moorland, beyond the tracks and daily life. He retreated to contemplate God, or whatever devil it was that drove him, and he was rarely seen in the village.

So their days continued on a predictable protectory until they reached early September, and without understanding why, things started to fall apart.

The first crack was a casual comment from Frederick when they had finished frolicking in the leaves. The two lay panting side by side, staring up at the wooded canopy and holding hands. Abigail wasn't sure she would ever be as happy as she was today. Frederick sat up, adjusting his clothes to make himself respectable again. "I'd better not be too late back. Don't want mother worrying about me as well."

"Your mother need not worry," Abigail murmured. She didn't think Mrs Flintoff would have any issue with her.

"Maisie's been gone two days."

"Gone where?"

"We don't know."

Abigail opened her eyes. "She's disappeared?"

"I doubt it. She'll be away over with James somewhere. Wouldn't surprise me if she comes back wed."

"Who is James?"

Frederick laughed. "You don't pay much attention to folk, do you, my love? James is her sweetheart, has been for months."

"Oh."

A simple oh was the start of it. A touch of unease. A breath of air and a turning hinged upon it. They said without the suffering one could not appreciate those flickerings of happiness one had in this mortal life. They were like glimmers of a feeling one could look forward to in heaven. If one was good enough. All things changed. Accept the impermanence of life.

The following evening, the young man Abigail had never paid all that much attention to, James, who hailed from a farming hamlet of Oulston, appeared in Kilburn with a harried look about him. Up until that point the family had been angry with Maisie for running off with her sweetheart and neglecting to tell anyone, but they were not too anxious. She wasn't a particularly silly girl and the worst that might have happened was that she had gotten in the family way, and would return married. The worst that could have happened - her mother would weep bitterly over that phrase long into the night. James had heard word that Maisie had left home without a word several days ago to be with him. Which would have been wonderful had it been true, but James had not seen her since Sunday last. They had met in the woods as usual – he had the decency to blush a little at this point in front of her parents – and parted later, he to take the long walk back to Oulston, she down the bank to return to Kilburn. After much discussion between the family and neighbours, it was decided that no one had seen Maisie since.

Maisie knew those woods too well to get lost. And although it was possible for a couple to have some quiet privacy in a dell somewhere, there were too many folk about for anyone to fall and hurt themselves and not be noticed. The men set out at once with long sticks to search as much of the woodland as possible before the light failed them. Her mother cried. One neighbouring housewife shook her head and started to mutter that the fairy folk had taken Maisie until she was silenced by a sharp look. It was hardly helpful when the girl had vanished and the family was in distress, but women knew they had to mind themselves. The execution of a number of local midwives and unpopular women a few years ago had calmed the fever, but edicts from the king and news from neighbouring counties were starting to stir at discontent. People needed someone to blame.

Abigail left the Flintoff home as dusk was thickening, trudging up towards Kilburn Hall with worry dragging after her. She saw the men come out of the forest as the light was almost gone. Grim and upright, with no invalid or body as their cargo.

Mrs Cook was still up when she returned to the kitchens. Grimacing, with her swollen red ankle upon a milking stool in front of the fire, she was drinking some tea she had just brewed, having waited until the current Martha had gone away to bed. She didn't want to risk Martha asking silly questions about what Mrs Cook had been putting in the pot. She jumped guiltily when the door went, and on seeing Abigail-Mary would have relaxed only that the jolt had unsettled her painful leg.

Abigail glanced at the leg. It looked bad, and she knew Mrs Cook wasn't treating it as she ought to. "You need a compress on that," she muttered.

"You ought not to have loose hair out of that cap," Mrs Cook snapped back. She held a scowl for a few moments then softened when she saw the look of worry on Abigail's face. "Don't mind me. I don't suppose anyone notices this time of night. I have had a compress on it, when I have chance. Can't say as I want folks to notice."

"You need to stay off it for a few days."

Mrs Cook raised her eyebrows. "And that I can't do either. I don't want folks noticing else they'll be sending for the doctor, and I don't want quackery done to me."

"I doubt the master would notice."

"Aye, but the mistress would. I can sort this myself."

They fell into silence, listening to the flames crackle. The unspoken fact that they could treat it properly, if they had the freedom to do as they wished. If they did not need to worry over being watched, or being accused of nonsense by people who knew no better.

"You been over with the Flintoffs again?" Mrs Cook asked, trying to sound casual. Everyone knew Frederick was courting Abigail, and they would probably be wed not all that far away. It gave her hope, to think that a serving maid out of this place might actually be able to leave service without having been taken advantage of by the masters. That someone might actually get their happy end.

Abigail nodded slowly. "Maisie's gone missing. No one's seen her since Sunday."

"Maisie? The pretty one?" Mrs Cook knit her brows. "I hear she has a sweetheart a few villages over. She'll be with him."

"No," Abigail whispered. "He got word of it, it reached over Oulston way, and he came over this evening. He's not seen her since Sunday. He was probably the last to see her."

Mrs Cook paled. "You don't think he did anything to her?"

"James?" Abigail looked shocked by the suggestion that one person could do such a terrible thing to another. Her naivety could be rather comical given all that she had been through and witnessed in her young life. "No, I can't believe it."

"Neither can I," Mrs Cook's countenance darkened. "You mind yourself wherever you go now, Mary, you understand. These are dark times for young women."

"Do you think she's gone to the fairy folk."

"I do not." Mrs Cook cut her short. "And I don't want to hear such nonsense coming from you again. And certainly not in the hearing of anyone but me." She looked down at her hands around her empty cup. The heat from the hot tea had dispersed and she felt a chill. "I've a bad feeling about this, Mary," she said quietly. "I hope she's dead."

"But Maisie's such a good young woman, honest, Mrs Cook. She wouldn't do..."

"Hush now, lass. I bear her no ill will. I just think death may be preferable to some of the other things that might have happened."

"What do you..."

"Never you mind," she waved Abigail-Mary off with her hand. "Away to bed with you. There's a whole new day of chores tomorrow."

The day started particularly early. Much to be done, and hardly any staff for the stable boys and gardeners had been sent over to Thirsk to collect a large shipment for the master. Martha was upstairs attending to the mistress before the day was light. She was struggling with another pregnancy. Mrs Cook pursed her lips and muttered to herself that she had never known a woman to suffer such bruising from pregnancy. She had been ready to rant away in her private fury before she caught Abigail-Mary stumbling in with half sleep in her eyes, and sent her off to light the fire in the main hall.

Abigail-Mary had cleaned out the fireplace and taken the ashes out to the garden herself, as the men were away. She had dumped them in the ash pile, watching the wind whisp small fragments away, before remembering she still had a list to complete before breakfast, and hurried back inside, only just remembering to take fresh firewood with her.

On her knees before the fire, she leant forward as if about to go down in supplication to the gods. No adoration required, just an arrangement of the firewood and kindling to get a steady fire going quickly. She felt a dull, hard thump against her rear end, and her first thought was that the fire poker must have somehow toppled over and hit her on the behind. She glanced across and saw it was still in its stand. She shuffled slightly to nudge the object away, but when it clasped her buttock through her skirts she realised it wasn't a what but a who.

She'd thought all the stable lads and garden boys had gone, but perhaps one had been left behind and was taking advantage of the lack of supervision to creep about and tease the maids. As she twisted to whack him away, the hand tightened its grip and pushed her forward into the dormant fire. Abigail-Mary let out a gasp in panic, and reached out for a block of firewood to knock her assailant over the head.

Just as she was about to strike, Mrs Cook's irritated voice came echoing from the entrance hall. "Mary, will you get here now!" she shouted. "I've been shouting you these last five minutes. Do I have to come and drag you out here?"

The pressure on her rear end suddenly disappeared. Abigail-Mary scrambled to her feet in a rising twist. The rough, splintered piece of log was still in her hand. She was momentarily stunned to see Montague Angehard swiftly, but casually moving to the other side of the room. He stopped by the table and stared down at the serving girl with a mix of disgust and ownership. Abigail-Mary's mind caught up with itself and she realised he had meant to do to her what he and his father, and that oafish brother, had done to all of the other Martha's over the years.

"Time you were a mere maid no longer."

Abigail-Mary stood tall, throwing the log back onto the unlit fire with a hollow clatter. How dare he? She would not be another drowned girl in a pond. She had her life planned with Frederick.

Montague returned the stare, and for a moment there was a standoff, before an irritated blush reddened his face. "Are you questioning your lord and master, girl?" he barked. "Get back to work."

"Mary!" Mrs Cook shouted.

Abigail-Mary darted out of the room into the entrance hall, surprised to find that Mrs Cook wasn't already there raging with thunder to drag her back to the kitchen. Running down the passage she came to Mrs Cook leaning heavily in the kitchen doorway. She caught the older woman before she tried to walk any further. Her ankle was so swollen that taking any more than a couple of steps was too much.

"Oh, Mrs Cook."

"Don't you Mrs Cook me, girl. Where were you?"

"I was..." Abigail-Mary flustered and lost her words. She looked at the older woman and felt her eyes grow moist. She shook her head. "I was trying to get the fire set and he..."

Mrs Cook's eyes widened. "Say no more. Nothing...?"

Abigail-Mary shook her head.

"Oh my girl, we must go careful. It is probably for the best I need to send you out just now. I will have to had a think."

Abigail-Mary helped her hobble across to the stool by the kitchen fire. "I need to help you in here today."

"You can when you get back. But the lads are all gone and that basket should have gone yesterday." She pointed at a wicker basket full of provisions on the end of the kitchen table. "I would not wish to send you up to that awful place, but I can't so much as walk to the end of the manor myself, and the lads are all away today."

"What awful place?"

"His hermitage."

Henry Angehard and his strange little stone cell of solitude. Supposedly pious and godly, yet whenever anyone mentioned it, there was a disturbed hushed look that fell from people's brows. The hermitage. Abigail knew where it was, but she had not gone to see the building.

"You set that basket on the ground outside the door," Mrs Cook gave her instruction. "Knock heavily on the door with a stick or stone, make sure he hears it. Then you leave."

"You don't wait?"

Mrs Cook shook her head, "You get moving straight away, and under no circumstance are you to enter that building, do you understand? No matter what he says, if you've the misfortune to see him. Just get away."

"All right," Abigail-Mary said slowly, uncertain as to what Mrs Cook was so frightened of. Henry Angehard was terrified of women, he was hardly a threat. Not like his elder brother. She slipped her hand under the basket handle, and picked it up, resting it in the crook of her elbow. It was heavier than expected. This must be at least a week of provisions.

"Get going before he starts trying to catch you again," Mrs Cook advised, "and when you're back, straight into the kitchen to me. We'll have to think as to what to do longer term. I promised your grandmother..." she stopped, raising her eyebrows at the young woman. "Are you deaf? Away with you now."

Abigail-Mary nodded, and hurried out of the back doorway into the yard. She moved fast and low through the garden edges and out of the walled gardens by a narrow gate. She stopped as she stepped out onto the path with that sudden sensation that she was being watched in close quarters. She turned, eyes darting, before she settled on the sparkling little black rat eyes watching her from the top of an old broken fence post. The rat, a dark brown female, and one of Abigail's pets, stood up on its hind legs and sniffed at the air.

"You're wanting to come with me? I'm sure it'll be no bother."

The rat stood up a little straighter.

"I don't have the time to argue." Abigail hurried up to the fencepost and opened up her apron pocket so the rat could leap in. "It'll be too long a walk for you, so best you catch a ride."

The rat squeaked and curled up for a rest, as Abigail started a swift march to the forests and hillsides that would lead her up onto the open-topped moors. As she disappeared into the tree line, sensing the dappled shadows of the canopy filter across her body, she felt her nerves subside. A sensation of wellbeing and safety enveloped her. A long walk through forest and moorland. She couldn't understand why no one wanted to pick up this task.

Up on the wild open moors, where the wind blew more often than it did not, Abigail-Mary followed the age-old safe track between the sphagnum bogs and deceptive patches of thick, soupy peat-earth that would gladly suck a man under. Fall into the arms of the earth and sleep. This was a lonely corner of the moors, going over the horizon and falling out of sight of any building or settlement, bar that strange stone building recently erected by the Angehards.

The setting looked as most other patches of the moors, with the heather, the bogs, and the wind whipping across the tops. Yet one did not hear the birds, and the wild-roaming sheep did not linger if they made the mistake to stray this way. There was a creeping sensation of something watchful and unpleasant. Abigail recalled Mrs Cook's advice to set the basket down at the door and immediately walk away. Now she was here, she knew she would do it without needing to be asked. In her apron, the rat was increasingly unsettled, writhing and squeaking.

The hermitage was a miserable squat building, hunched up in its own secret guilt. Stone work with a thick heather roof to try and make it blend and settle in the landscape. Yet the moors rejected it, and it seemed to hover unaccepted by the ground, dank and foreboding. If this was what it was to contemplate God, one might wonder what appeal religion would have for anyone. Perhaps such destitution only increased the appeal of heaven even more. Anyone who could serve God here must be deserving of their eternal rewards.

There was an unpleasant, squalid smell emanating from the building. There were dark holes for windows at the bottom, perhaps to air the floors or keep the cellar fresh. They stared like dead eyes. Abigail had to avert her gaze as she hurried up the side of the building through the cleared heather where signs of recent construction still lay. Around the corner she was thankful to see the door, a solid wooden rectangle of prison function. A block of sandstone had been dug into the earth at the foot of the door to serve as a doorstep. In the wettest part of winter, it would be very boggy here. The cellar would probably fill. Perhaps that was why the slit windows were there, as an overflow facility. Abigail set the basket down, feeling the release of strain on her arm. The rat was scrabbling at her thigh through her skirts. She did not wish to stay.

She glanced over her shoulder, as if expecting a spectre with extended claw. A sharp, short hammer on the door, then Abigail was gone in a swirl of skirts, fleeing straight for the deep heather that would tug at her clothes. Here it almost felt as if it was pushing her away. Nothing would hold her back.

When she was a distance from the hermitage, she paused to look back. A sad whimper came out of the air.

"Abigail."

Abigail's brow creased. She pulled back her cap, freeing her ear to the wind. There was no voice, no sound, but she was sure she had heard her name. She dropped her eyes, and saw the brown rat stood tall, staring at her out of the apron pocket. "Have you learned to speak now?" she whispered.

The rat squeaked and tried to jump up. There was a bang of an opening door, then a questioning voice from the hermitage. Abigail let her feet go out from under her and dropped into the cover of the heather, pulling her skirts down from the scratchy dried branches. The wind dropped as she disappeared into shelter, wrenching off her white cap so that her own dark chestnut hair would camouflage her into the moors.

At the hermitage, an unwashed haggard Henry Angehard picked up the basket of provisions, before walking to the side of the building to stare out across the moors. He called out, asking where they were, for it had only been a moment since he'd heard the bang on the door. From here he could see for miles, and there was no sign of another human. He circled the building, feeling wary of being observed. There was no one, yet one of those stable lads must be hunkered down in the heather somewhere, watching him. Insolent brats. Scowling, he returned to his hermitage, slamming the door after him.

Abigail waited some time before she dared to get up and run out of sight of the hermitage. The heather seemed to part for her, and she was soon away and heading back for the forested bank sides to get back to Kilburn.

Cook glanced up from her seat by the fire when Abigail-Mary returned. Her leg was propped up on a stool. It had not been an easy few hours whilst she had been a maid less. The master had been down, actually into the kitchen, to complain of a fire place that was not as clean as he liked. The maid needed to come and see to it now. Now, he had demanded. Mrs Cook had been at the table, setting down the knife from the leaves she had been cutting, and said she would attend to it herself. The squire had looked furious, on the brink of saying he wouldn't want an old hag like her coming through. He held his tongue. Mrs Cook had been there long enough to know the turnover of maids. But he would not have his authority questioned by an old woman. Get the maid to do it, he said. She's out at the hermitage with supplies, had been Mrs Cooks response. The squire had inwardly cursed Henry and his nonsense. The sooner he caught a chill in that pit of his and died, the better. No matter, he had decided, when he had seen Mrs Cook make to move. The day was not too cold, and he did not think he would use the room today.

Mrs Cook gazed sadly at Abigail-Mary. They were going to have to get canny very quickly if she was to keep Abigail-Mary away from the fate of every other maid of Kilburn Hall. "My girl," she sighed. "There are two sheets still hanging outside. I think it will be damp tonight. Would you bring them in?"

Out in the drying yard Abigail-Mary unpegged the sheets and folded them up. The ironing would wait until tomorrow. Setting them in a laundry basket, she looked across to the coal shed where she had set down the brown rat on an upturned box. She stood on her haunches, her black eyes piercing and unblinking as she stared at Abigail. Three other rats had joined her on the box. Waiting.

Abigail crouched down before her friends. "Will you not talk to me again?" she asked, wondering if it could be so that she had really heard the voice of the rat. The beasts stared at her. The brown female lifted her nose to something in the air, twitching her whiskers.

Five more rats came out of a hole at the bottom of the coal shed door. Abigail lowered her eyes. She wanted to go to sleep. "You want me to go back there?"

Two of the rats jumped down from the box and joined the five from the coal shed. They ran, fury bodies rippling in the as they made for the gate as if to head for the forest. They stopped, rising on their back legs to look questioningly at Abigail.

"I can't now, Mrs Cook has a list of chores waiting for me. Her leg's bad and I'll have extra to do. I'll be so tired come this evening." Abigail said as the brown female hopped back into her apron pocket.

"You're not taking no for an answer, are you," she sighed. "All right. This evening, when my work is done. It's to be a clear moon this evening and it will guide our way."

Darkness seethed about the hermitage like a silent mist. Abigail crested a rise on the moorland and regarded the squat building. They were position in a standoff, the great heap of stonework containing something dreadful, facing a young woman and countless rats. Abigail didn't know who they were or why they had joined the party. She didn't normally attract the attention of woodland creatures. A silent, common understanding must have swept through the local rat population, for they were all here. Her pets had travelled in her apron pockets. The others had run with her, sometimes leaping over one another to sweep over high bushels of heather, or cutting twisting runs through the gnarled branches and shoots of the scrub coming from the peaty earth.

The clouds shifted wind-blown over the inky sky, releasing the full gloaming of the moon. Ivory highlights slipped across the contours of the hermitage. A night breeze rustled through the heather, rattling reed stems together in open patches of ground. Abigail brushed her hair from her face. She had taken off her bonnet, for it was too light coloured and she did not wish to stand out in the night. Her natural colours were better suited to this landscape. Really she ought to have asked herself why she was even making this journey. Why now? She couldn't vocalise it. Just an animal instinct.

The rodents started down towards the lonely building, Abigail following by wading through the heather with ease. As they approached the stench grow worse, stronger than she recalled from earlier in the day. Misery, piss, human effluence. Void of hope. The rats scrambled out of her pocket and dropped like stones to the ground, their bodies rippling in racing as they ran over the clearing towards the base of the side wall. There was an opening, a window, a vent at the bottom where the chewed up mud was starting to settle against the eruption of the wall. A foul stink was drifting out from that black rectangular slit. The rats ran towards it, gathering at either side, sitting up on their haunches and waiting. The brown female looked back for Abigail.

Dropping to her hands and knees, grimacing her mouth into a closed line to try and avoid the worst of the smell, Abigail crept up to the opening. She felt her face go red, the blood rushing to the skin as if protection from the reek. Her hands slid in the grimy earth. She scooped a handful of churned mud away from the opening to make it a perfect rectangle. She glanced at the rat, who could barely be seen in this shadow, only the sparkling of her eyes. "What are we looking at here?" She whispered.

There was a gasp, a dying, barely sounded gasp from within. Without colour and vision, a gauge of distance was unattainable. It might had been metres away just as it might have been by her ear. Abigail scuffled back in horror. She lurched up on her haunches, far enough back should a monster crook a gnarled claw out of that slit it could not drag her down into the belly of hell. One of the rats squeaked. There was a shuffling noise, and something, someone on the inside, moved across a room. There was the slightest hint of an object beyond the yawning opening of the slit. Then it hoarsely whispered her name. "Abigail."

Abigail darted forward again. The voice sounded aged, beat in, and for a moment she thought of her grandmother, although what the old woman would be doing in the belly of the hermitage she couldn't even guess at. She roughly dug in at the ground and wrenched out of fistful of dirt, giving that slit a deep sagging belly. The vaguest hint of a head within the shadows, pressed up against the other side of the opening, broke the pure black. Then fingers appeared in the opening. Filth smeared, pale and desperate. But not old.

She reached in and touched the fingers, and didn't panic when the hand clutched desperately at hers. Her eyes widened as she realised she had just made contact with Frederick's sister.

"Maisie?"

"Oh," the young woman wept, her voice strained. "Oh Abigail, I am lost."

"Why are you..."

"He stole me away. I never...." Another hand joined the first as she desperately clung to Abigail's fingers. "You must tell them all I never abandoned them. But I cannot get out."

"I'll go get help," Abigail started, thinking of Frederick, of James. Those strong young men would have her out of here. This time tomorrow..."

"He'd kill me before you go back," Maisie whispered. "It's all lost."

Abigail felt her bile rise. Not again. She thought of the Martha locked up in the prison wagon. The pregnant Martha certain she'd been lady of the manor, but ended up drowned in the mire. Her own mother hanged for the crime of compassion. "I can't..."

The brown rat squeaked and a couple of the furry bodies darted down through the slit and into the prison. Maisie shrieked as she felt the little bodies run down her ragged skirts, using her frame as a bridge, and disappear into the darkness to explore the cell.

"They won't hurt you," Abigail whispered.

"What will we do?" Maisie sobbed. "Will you bring me something to kill myself."

"That's a sin!"

"And this isn't?"

"I'll get James."

"There's no time. And who would want me after.... After all this?"

The girls clung to one another's fingers, heads lowered in the darkness. They were deaf to the sound of movement above, until there was a bang higher up. "Girl, what noise are you making down there?"

Maisie squeaked in panic, an automatic reaction of flesh horrified by memory. Of future knowledge. "Oh I can't do this again," she sobbed.

Abigail started to cry in frustration. What was a foolish young girl, a kitchen maid, supposed to do? She couldn't battle a man, her social superior. She'd end up in the stocks, or worse. Her fingers dug into the earth, rats started to pour down through the window. She could hear Maisie whirling in panic. There must have been a door in the ceiling, for a chink of distant candlelight radiated down as a panel was lifted. Maisie screamed. Abigail started to dig in a frenzy, wishing she were a rabbit or a badger or anything, only something that had the power and the technique to dig quickly.

"You, wrench," Henry's voice boomed, angry at being disturbed from his sleep. "You disturb your master? You have not learned your lesson."

"Oh no, please leave me," Maisie sobbed.

It started to rain outside, the earth swiftly growing slick as Abigail dug with her hands. Inside Masie wept and screamed. Henry started down the steps to the cell. He was quoting bible verse at her. He said he was trying to drive away the devil. Then he was distracted, hitting and swearing before he too started to scream. The noise was matched in the squealing of the woodland rats. Abigail felt nauseous, as if she might pass out. To her side the brown rat sat calmly, overseeing proceedings. She sensed grunting and a musty smell. Abigail looked in confusion when she discovered a badger digging at one side, rabbits at the other. Earth was flying up in a spoil heap behind them.

Before the gap was big enough Maisie's grimy arms were already flailing outside. Abigail grabbed her by the upper arms, shocked by how lose the flesh on her bones felt, and started to pull. Maisie dug her knees and her feet into the wall as she scrambled up, heaving her weary torso into the hole. Her face and grease-drenched filthy hair emerged into the moonlight, a babe born of horror. Abigail got her hands under the girl's armpits, gritted her teeth and heaved until Maisie came bursting out of the earth hole to the soundtrack of a screaming man, both girls slick with wet earth, blood and filth. Gasping, Maisie rolled off Abigail and sprawled on her back, gulping in deep draughts of free, clean moorland air. She had not thought she would ever come out of there alive.

Abigail sat up, watching as rats started to emerge from the hole. Some had blood-slick faces, one had a broken leg. They hurried and fled, forgetting the group and the mission, dispersing to the moorland and heading for the forests again. Anguished cries from the monster echoed out from the black. The candle light had been snuffed out.

"We have to get away from here. Can you walk?"

"I will," Maisie said, wobbling on her legs and clutching at Abigail for support. "I want my Mamma."

"You can't go home," Abigail whispered, holding the shaking girl by the shoulders and dragging her away from the hermitage. "It's too dangerous. Come away, oh come away."

"Mamma!" Maisie wept.

"We'll get away to somewhere safe," Abigail whispered. "Then we'll think what to do." It was an empty reassurance, for Abigail was not sure they could do anything. They could never speak of what had happened, the Angehard family wouldn't stand for it, no matter how much Henry was scorned. The damage could not be undone.

The girls ran and stumbled, sometimes barely staggering, but always moving away across the moors, until dawn. Maisie blindly followed, Abigail supported her weight, not thinking where they ought to go or what would be the best thing to do. She couldn't think beyond the next ten footsteps.

Eventually they arrived at the moorland stone circle. The same one Abigail's own grandmother had brought her to years ago.

Had she been asked to walk to it from the Hermitage, she might have struggled to come up with a direct route. It had just happened that they came here. The girls collapsed, Maisie sobbing for her mother. In the gloam of dawn a mizzle splattered across them, running tired lines through the dirt and filth on their skin. Like digging rabbits, they broke down through the uneven blanket of heather, to take shelter from wind and sight, down on the peaty ground. There they curled together and fell asleep.

Hours later Abigail woke, the first thought was Mrs Cook. She ought to have started work hours ago, and no one would have found her. Mrs Cook would have sent the stable lad around the garden and the like to look for her. No Mary. Perhaps a panic might set in that she had run away, that the master had managed to catch up with her. Mrs Cook wouldn't know whether to cry or fume, but she would have to put on a performance of irritation for the benefit of others. Word might get out into the village, and then there would be two missing girls.

Maisie coughed. She had been awake for some time, her brain trying to process all that had happened. Her face was a mottle of bruises and filth, things that would heal and wash away on the surface. "I never said anything to him," she whispered.

Abigail twisted to look her friend in the eye. "Who?"

"The squire's brother. I've never had any dealings with him. I don't why he..." she faltered, unsure how to put it into words. What had happened, what he had done.

But he had been watching you, Abigail thought. Like a magpie and a shiny coin and he had decided he would have you. A sickening bile rolled in her stomach. That cellar, that pointless cellar in the hermitage. Is that why he had built the place, for the solitude of abuse?

"I can't go back to the village," Maisie whispered. "I want Mamma but I can't go back. What can I tell people? No one will believe me, not against the squire's kin."

Abigail closed her eyes, thinking of the common women who had stood up to the Angehards. Dear Martha. Or the women who had not even stood up to the nobility, but simply gone about their lives, and caught attention. Women who had been branded witches. A word from a man and the suspicion was cast upon a woman for life. A demand from an Angehard and a noose would be about her neck. "Perhaps he will be ashamed and say nothing." Even as she said it, she did not believe it.

"What if he took me back?"

That was a strong possibility. Abigail's eyes snapped open. "I'll go back to Kilburn today," she said. "We'll hide you, and I'll go back. See what's happening. It'll be safe for me." She sat up from the nest of heather. "I'll get word to James, he'll come."

Maisie started to weep again, shaking her head. "No he won't. He won't have me. I'm damaged now."

"You'll heal."

"He did things to me," Maisie's whisper was so low it could barely be heard. Melting into the breeze a moment after speaking. "Things only a man should do with his wife. And even then, worse things. Things they say the devil does to his witches. No one wants a lass who has been taken. They all want pure maids."

"Were you a pure maid before?"

Maisie glanced down, wiping the loose snot from her nose. "No, but that doesn't change it, does it?"

"What he did to you? No, it doesn't." Abigail's mouth formed a hard line. "But James is a good man and I think we should not assume man's sins are on all men." She stood up and looked across the moorland. She couldn't see anyone else. "Can you walk? We'll get away to somewhere you can hide, then I'll go back. I'll see what's doing, and I'll send word to James."

"Where will we go first? I don't want to stay here all day."

"Grandmother told me there were caves on Black Hambleton Hill. You can hide there."

Maisie looked horrified. "But isn't it haunted?"

"Only to them that deserve it," Abigail muttered. She offered her hand. "I'll come with you, we'll find a cave, then I'll get back to Kilburn as quick as I can."

Maisie looked terrified. "I'm to wait alone? What if he finds me?"

"You'll be safe," Abigail told her. "I'll come back tonight. Fear not."

Maisie sobbed as if the world had ended. It was the second night. Perhaps the immensity of the rest of her life was settling in her consciousness. The surreal awfulness of what had happened was past but still flashing in her memory. Perhaps the tears were just relief. There was a possibility of a future. She would not have to live in this dank cave forever, or return to Kilburn and face whatever retribution the gossips and the nobles felt fitting. And there would be retribution if she ever returned.

Abigail sat outside of the cave in the heather, her arms hugging her knees as she gazed westward and watched the sun sink. Its red glow was streaked by lines of seemingly stationary clouds. A glowing dying orb. To be reborn the next day. Before then we shall be cast into darkness. She lowered her eyes to her hands, trying to ignore the mutterings between James and Maisie as he calmed her. At least he had not rejected her, which many a man would have done, worried over the destroyed virginity, or the dirty shame of where another man had trespassed. He had even worked things out for their future, for he had an uncle up in the Dales where they could go. James could get a job on the farm, start rearing some of his own flocks of sheep there to amass a little money. Maisie could work as a dairy maid and be safe. Then in a year or two they could be married. They couldn't come back, but they could start fresh, live at liberty and not have to watch their backs.

James might have felt the need to watch his back for a little time at Oulston, but that would have been all. Maisie would have had no hope. Abigail-Mary had returned to the manor house late in the morning. Mrs Cook hadn't uttered a word but her sharp eyes had been questioning. She suspected Mary was hiding from the Lord of the Manor, now in the latest game of cat and mouse that no girl had ever won in the end. As they'd been tidying the kitchen after the luncheon, Mrs Cook had let out a great sigh. "I'll miss you, Mary," she spoke. "You've been here with me a long time but I think it's time for you to be moving on."

Abigail-Mary felt a panic pinch her stomach. There was nowhere else she could work in Kilburn and she did not want to move to far from Frederick.

Mrs Cook smiled sadly at her expression. "I wasn't necessarily saying you should seek a job elsewhere. I've been very content with your work. Only he will catch you sooner or later and you'll end up the way of all the other Martha's." She paused. "I hear on the local gossip, not that I pay much mind, that you and Frederick Flintoff may have an understanding? I would say it might be prudent to get wedded before the year is out."

She felt a blush rise up on her face. It surprised her as she usually didn't feel embarrassed. "We have spoken of maybe..."

"I'd hurry his maybe into a date." Mrs Cook advised.

Any further discussion ceased for the lady of the house, heavily pregnant and lumbering ungainly, hurried into the kitchen, searching desperately for practical women. For people paid to do what they were told, for she could not face to do what was asked. "Oh Mrs Cook," she gasped.

"Mistress," Mrs Cook almost dropped the bowl she was holding on the flagstone floor. "What has happened? It's not your time yet surely?"

"No, it's not me. It's the squire's brother. He's just turned up. He's in a dreadful state, been beaten by thieves I would guess. I've sent a lad for the doctor, but could you come now and help?"

"Mary, get me some hot water," Mrs Cook asked as she followed the lady of the house to the front of the house.

The younger brother, Henry, must have trudged across the moors for the best part of the morning, heaving and gasping, half blind as he staggered down through the woodland. A dying beast searching for home. His robes were ripped savagely, gore and piss drenched. His entire head was shredded and bloody, and seemingly covered in clumps. As Mrs Cook started to wash at the man's face in tentative dabs, darting back as the screaming and flailing started. It was obvious this was not a regular beating. Clumps of the man's face and scalp were missing, as if he were half eaten. Worse, what they thought had been a clump of hair plastered over an eye with dry blood, proved to be matted hair plastered over an empty eye socket, the opening ripped and wrenched from the meat of his face as if something had tried to clamber in. The squire's initial irritation at his younger brother's womanly sobbing and drama from a little beating, turned to breathless horror as the household began to see the extent of his wounds.

"What in God's name?"

Henry wrenched back his head. Mrs Cook's ministrations had triggered off nerve pulsations. He was in agony afresh. He flailed on the table where he'd half collapsed, half been flung by the gardeners, like a dying eel. The one bloodied eye sought out his brother. "Witches."

The squire's face hardened. "I drove them all out with father years ago. We cleared the nest." Wrinkling his face with disgust, he lent in closer to his mangled brother. "Perhaps we missed one? Or one has since grown up."

His brother grabbed at his sleeves with surprising strength. Agony bringing power to tendons. He hung on. "Maisie," he gargled.

Abigail-Mary was in the shadows, and felt the breath catch in her throat as she heard the name. The words had been spoken, his defence thrown into the court before any accusations could be made. He was nobility and a godly man. One who had been visibility attacked and spoke and named witches. No one would believe Maisie had been taken against her will and locked up to be raped and abused until she perished. She was dead if she came back to the village.

She and Frederick had gone up to the cave that evening. They'd sent word to James via one of the Flintoff brothers that he was to come the next day. Maisie's mother had been told she was safe, and not to believe any rumours that might come out in the next few days. But that Maisie could not come back and the family could not speak of it. She couldn't go to her daughter now, for the family would be watched for a time, and as a goodwife and a mother, she was not at liberty to go wandering as a man might. She would have to bide her time, then go out to visit Jame's uncle in the Dales when things had settled. Maisie had sobbed when she had been told of all of this. She so desperately wanted her mother's comfort. Her good name was linked with the devil at home and she had never done a thing wrong. None of this was her fault.

Frederick had been furious when Abigail had first told him. He was out to wreck revenge, on the squire or his brother at the hermitage or to report them somewhere. It had taken persuasion to hold him back. To face the reality of their powerlessness. It was possibly not something he had really faced before today, but Abigail had understood her place in the world for years. She could already see the futility of trying to right the wrongs. He eventually calmed, and their told his mother. Everyone agreed that it was best if father didn't know for now.

Now on Hambleton Hill, in the dying light, Frederick came out of the cave and sat down next to Abigail in the rough clouds of heather. "We don't have enough words to thank you for all you have done."

Abigail closed her eyes, breathed in his presence.

"Maisie will be safe. I'm going to travel with her to James' Uncle's farm. James will follow in a month. He's given notice at Oulston. I'll be sad to see them go, but glad they are safe."

She opened her eyes. "Mrs Cook thinks I need to move on."

"They don't know you have a role in all this?"

"I don't think so. I didn't hear him speak my name. He didn't see me at the hermitage." She paused. "But it's the squire. You remember how the Marthas at the house were always getting in trouble. In the family way?"

"Oh yes. I know there was a rumour that the squire might have been involved."

"No might about it. His eye is roving now that his wife is with child again. There's only so long I can play mouse to his cat."

"He's bothering you?"

Abigail looked woefully at him. "I don't want to end up with his bastard, drowning in the mire."

"It won't come to that."

"It might if I stay."

He threaded his fingers through hers. "Look, it's a bit earlier than I had planned, but if you and I were wed…"

Abigail grinned at him.

"It would solve that problem would it not?" They put their foreheads together. He tightened his clasp on her hand. That the Angehards would take everything, that they viewed the entire village, the buildings, the animals, the people as their mere playthings. But some good might come of it, if it brought forward his marriage to Abigail. They could stay with his parents until he had a home ready.

"I think that would be very nice."

"Nice," Frederick laughed. "I hope it will be more than nice."

"Wonderful, then. It's the only thing I had hopes for," she leant into him, pressing her nose and lips to the side of his face. "Perhaps good things will work out of all this awfulness."

Henry died a week later. The fever had consumed him. The bloodlettings, incense and other quack theories did nothing to bring the temperature down. Neither that nor the voluminous excretions of puss and infection that poured out of the chewed bite wounds, the gouges of missing flesh. The bloodied gaping hole from once he had seen. Swollen and yellow, ever growing to come slopping out of the eye socket. Sweat and puss soaked the sheets. Rancid stinking blood stains streaked down the off-white fabric. Mrs Cook kept a kettle of water on the constant boil to wash the soiled clothes and sheets as they came down on a regular cycle. They couldn't get things cleaned, dried and ironed quick enough to keep up with demand. Mrs Cook would shake her head and she and Mary-Abigail would exchange a look. Mrs Cook knew who Mary's mother had been, and no doubt the girl had picked up something before she had been sent away from the family home and into service. They knew what brew would bring down a fever. What could treat infections. That the sphagnum moss of the moors would bind into a wound, draw out the badness. But they could not speak it. For if it did not work, and not all souls and wounds were meant to be saved, they would be charged with witchcraft. Rumours were already set in stone that the harm Henry had suffered was the work of witches. Devilry was about in the woodlands above Kilburn. The priest preached it so from the pulpit that Sunday just before Henry died. It was the same day he refused to read the banns for Frederick and Abigail in deference for their suffering nobility. All in all it would be a month before some semblance of normality returned and he would concede to their wishes.

The squire behaved as his position and society expected. He found himself in a filthy mood that Henry could cause so much trouble and inconvenience. That he had to listen to the fawning prattle of the locals, of other squires from the district. What an example to us all Henry had been. He had been a pathetic little worm, and very undeserving of such words. Worse, he had to listen to it all, and nod along sagely, as if his younger brother really was an example to them all. It put him in a bad mood, and the permanent disgusted scowl was translated as grief by those who knew no better.

As to how his brother had come by those wounds, he was still at a loss. There had been bite marks, a great number of them all over Henry's body. Small marks from a small creature, a rodent perhaps. The kind of gnawing one might see on a corpse or rotting vegetable matter that the local rats had found their way to. Or those prisoners who had been tortured with a desperate rat in a cage whose only escape was to eat their way through living matter. Put a desperate rat in a corner and it will do anything to fight for its life.

The damage inflicted upon Henry was the work of more than one beast. He had been no corpse when attacked, and he had not been in a prison. So how had it happened? The squire had since been to the hermitage, a miserably little stone cell with an unpacked basket of food, some now rotting, some eaten by the insects and mice. A pathetic plan for a life. He'd been a little surprised to discover the underground cell, including the means to restrain a human being. Self-flagellation? Henry had always been cowardly, so it was hard to believe, and besides, no one could lock themselves up alone. Then there was the almighty stink down there, of shit and piss, stale iron and terror. What devilry had Henry been up to, out here on the lonely moors where he would be answerable to no one, not even God? Perhaps he had picked the wrong victim, for in his delusional mutterings he had spoken of witches and witchcraft. Of a girl with power. Another time he had said the name Maisie, and at some point the Squire had made the connection with a village girl who had disappeared several weeks ago. She clearly wasn't at the hermitage, at least not now, and had not reappeared at the village. A she devil witch who had called upon Satan to save her and take his revenge on Henry's weak flesh? It was possible. He remembered the good work he had helped with when his father was still alive. They had rooted out the witches and shipped them down to York for trail and execution. They had rid their land of an evil. Perhaps childish remnants had remained that had since matured. A woman's mind was weak, and it would not take much persuasion from the devil to turn her head away from goodness and a woman's proper place. Henry was a meek coward, but perhaps this Maisie had bewitched him, driven him mad, and the only solution he'd found was to take and imprison her. Perhaps there had been some foolish notion of trying to save her soul. Well, look how that had ended. Eaten alive by her familiars, ripped to shreds by the claws of hell. Hopefully the witch had fled without infecting anyone, but they would have to remain vigilant.

The first time he attended the village church after his brother's death, the priest read out the banns. Village life was starting again. There were two couples betrothed. Women he had not heard of, one of the lads was a cartwright, the other was that carpenter with the withered, deformed arm. It was attached to his torso like a boiled chicken wing. As much as the deformed man revolted him, he had to acknowledge that despite the disability, the lad had grown up determined and was a hard and capable worker. But what woman would want such a freak of a man? Did she not fear what kind of children would be begot of such a union? These villagers were stupid though, especially the women.

It was at the end of the service, leaving the church and stepping through the churchyard, that he happened to look back and saw that carpenter, Frederick Flintoff, with their kitchen maid gazing adoringly at him. The priest had said Abigail Craister. Why would Mary shuffle in as though she had a chance? So desperate and clueless. It reminded him that he had unfinished business with the maid. Henry's pestilence had rather put him off his stride.

He'd been to see his wife, who was ready to give birth at any moment. She'd mentioned that they would soon be losing the maid, and she understood the banns had been read.

"They never mentioned a Mary."

His wife stared levelly at him for a moment, wondering if he really was that clueless. No, only utterly uninterested in the actual identity of any woman. "The maids have never been called Mary or Martha," she said. "I thought you realised your mother started the tradition. To save the family the need to learn new names all of the time."

He looked surprised. His wife was aware of a nuance he was not. "So Mary isn't Mary?"

"She certainly wasn't christened that. She's Abigail Craister."

He had thrown his cup of beer across the floor, provoking a shrieking fit from his wife. Mary, who avoided and denied him, he the squire of Kilburn, an example of strong and superior manhood. Mary, Abigail, whatever label the wench chose to take, had chosen a poor cripple over him. How dare she.

A wounded ego can be a dangerous thing, especially in a privileged man who had always been told he was superior. A man going through a confidence crisis as he listened to people fawn over his dead brother's memory - an incapable pervert who had to lock women up to have his way. A man who was aware his wife was more popular than he in the household. It was something that had started to dawn on him when he realised how much more she knew about the people, the surrounding community. She had listened when he had stood above the buzz of piffling nonsense. A man who was getting older. A man who felt gout in his foot. A man who watched the young men of the village and wondered when he had ceased to be one of the young stags. A man who needed to assert that he was the best. He would not be cast aside in favour of some poor cripple.

As circumstance foretold, an aged oak would be his means of declaring his true worth. The trusted oak of the great English kingdom. They had endured a long period of rain with high winds, and the tree had already been dying. The crown was long since an empty network of dead branches, barren and skeleton. Sickly leaves were still produced from some side branches, but that was all. As they said, what was under the surface mirrored above, and if the crown was dead, the anchoring rootball was probably equally in decay. The wind and a loosened boulder were the final catalyst to push the mighty oak over. It was a gasping, dying crash that woke the villagers in the witching hour. Many lurched up from their beds as if they could not breath. Only the sound of the wind howled outside the walls. No one could say what was different that had brought them from slumber. Abigail-Mary had opened her eyes, and stared at the black ceiling. She sensed that an old forest God had fallen. It left a void which would take some time to be refilled. Periods of transition were dangerous. A time when monsters might walk the earth.

In the morning the wind abated, the rain ceased and the sun came out. It felt like a rebirth. The fallen oak was soon discovered, tilted at an awkward downward angle on a slope with a silent threat of hurtling itself onwards. It was propped partially by a couple of silver birches. It would fall more yet and some work would be required to make the area safe. One of the woodsmen stood at the base of the tree, where great straggling roots gasped up to the clear sky. The overhead canopy of leaves were on the turn for autumn, encrusted with raindrops not yet evaporated. And behind the tree was a great rough hole where some of the roots had been wrenched from the earth. He pursed his lips, surprised that an oak would fall in such a way. Conifers perhaps, the shallow rooted trees could go over easy. But oaks were the long term guardians. They put down deep roots. Perhaps it was the slope of the bank, and the disease within the tree that had done it. He put a work-roughened hand on the trunk and gazed down the length of the tree.

"It'll take a few heavy horses to pull this one out," he mused.

The squire Angehard looked mildly put out, as if the man was suggesting he ought to arrange things. But he looked at the oak, his oak, and wondered if something magnificent could not be made for him.

"Do what you need to," he instructed. "I want the main trunk for carpentry. The branches for firewood for the manor house."

"Aye."

They looked down the forest, where a number of young men were coming, already anticipated for the work. Apprentice woodsmen, the carpenter and his lads. Including that cripple, who was carrying a long, large saw with another. He couldn't stay here in the company of that infernal lad. Scowling confirmation at the head woodsman, he walked away.

Frederick and the other lad set the saw down, and he approached the side of the great oak. "This one has been sick for some time."

"Aye, that it has. It were only a matter of time."

"He's wanting the trunk in one piece?"

The woodsman nodded. "We'll get the young'uns to work on chopping off branches. I reckon we're best off sawing through the trunk up near the roots."

Frederick looked along the length of the tree. "Lucky that rock is there under it. Otherwise the tree could go sliding."

The woodsman sniffed. "Now we want it moved, it'll be hard to budge."

By the late afternoon the tree was still where it had fallen. A lot of the branches had been lopped off, chopped up for firewood and basketed away from the site. The body of the tree had been severed from the roots and a great drift of sawdust surrounded the site like a froth of spores. As the team came to think on how they would get it out of the forest, the recently loosened rock that had been aiding turned into a hindrance. They had taken a number of poles and hammered them into the soft earth to hold the tree in place whilst they laboured to shift the rock out of the most direct route. When the heavy horses were brought up to tow the trunk out, the path needed to be as obstacle free as possible. They had managed to move the rock a couple of metres, but it was getting dug into the ground and trapped by other trees. The effort exerted felt fruitless. It was decided with the few yards of moving space, they would first get the horses to pull the trunk around to reangle it, before towing it away. One reached a point when one could push against a rock no longer.

They elected to take a break before the next phase. The woodsman and a couple of lads headed down to the village to see if the horses were ready. They didn't expect to get the old trunk to Kilburn today, but at least if they could see if the reangling would be possible, they could cease pondering on the problem of the boulder. Abigail passed the woodsman on her way up. She had been sent with a basket of refreshments from Mrs Cook.

She found Frederick sitting in a dry, warmed patch of sawdust by the tree smoking a pipe. Putting the basket down at the edge of the clearing, she broke out into a wide grin and hurried across to him.

Higher up on the bank, the Squire Angehard watched with increasing fury. His wife had never looked at him like that. And this maid, why ought she bother him so? She was not the only female in his domain. There was Martha as well. There was always a good turnover of maids. But this one had the very gall to cunningly avoid him whilst putting poison to his mind whilst he slept. And would chose a cripple, and a poor man instead. He spat into the undergrowth as the young couple held hands and sneaked away into the undergrowth. They were betrothed, they would soon be wed, and yet their lack of morals meant they would not wait.

He stomped down to the tree, stumbling and almost falling a couple of times. He would have some piece of mighty furniture made from this oak for the manor house. Perhaps a throne. He sniffed at the idea, and walked down the shaft of the tree, running a hand along the rough, aged bark until he came to the rough top where a number of posts stood to steady it. The ground was soft from the rainfall, and from the effort of shifting the boulder. Some of the posts looked loose. Shoddy workmanship. But what could one expect from a cripple? He heard a girlish giggle from the forest undergrowth, and felt his bile rise. In fury he wrenched one of the posts and threw it down. It felt so good that he did it with another, pleased that he had the strength to do it single handedly. The posts made a hollow clatter as he threw them down. Now the tree was held in place with only one, and perhaps it didn't even need that. He'd heard some groaning but there was no movement. It would hold.

Walking back up to the roots, he ignored the tree and went to examine the root crown. In comparison to the trunk and the branches one saw in the forest, this looked like an ugly, dirt-ridden mess. What would they do with this great disgusting tangle once the severed trunk had been removed?

Frederick Flintoff returned to the clearing, elated on the post coital glow. His smile soon dropped when he saw the posts lying on the ground. "Bloody hell," he swore, hurrying across. At first he assumed they had loosened and fallen over, but when he found them tossed in a pile like fire sticks, he realised they had been deliberately pulled. "Which blasted fool has been up to mischief here?"

Shadowed by the root crown, Montague Angehard's eyes flashed indignantly at the slur. He watched as the young carpenter stepped into the path of the trunk and bent down to retrieve one of the posts. How dare he. And he, a creature with a wizened piglet of an arm. I am the master here, he silently roared, and flung himself at the tree in anger. The impact was hard and unforgiving, and he would carry the bruises in his hip and his side for over a month. Bruises he would keep hidden.

The impact, that push was all that had been missing, and the tree started to move. Frederick straightened up, one pole grasped in his good hand as the mighty felled tree came sliding down the hillside at him. It moved at a surprising speed given it only went a few yards before being stopped by a well-wedged boulder. Frederick let out a dull groan, a wretch as if he was bringing up bile. The pole dropped from his hand and his head dropped down to look upon the crushed, bloodied mess that had once been his chest. He lifted his head, a mouth now splattered with crimson blood, and saw the horrified look of the Squire Angehard, who soon disappeared into the foliage of the forest. What had he been doing here, Frederick wondered, before he reflected that he couldn't feel his legs or arms.

Abigail let out a scream as she returned for her basket and discovered the tree moved and her love crushed between wood and rock. She ran for the tree as the younger lads playing in the forest on their break heard her screams and returned to the workplace. She couldn't get her thoughts straight, and her distressed cries came out in a garble of English. Emotions and demands. No no no. Not now. Not this. Frederick felt drunk, barely able to keep his head up. He couldn't feel his body, but he understood he was powering down, dying. Soon he would be with God. "I am sorry, Abigail," he whispered.

"No, oh no. Please don't." She scrabbled at him, her hands slick with blood as she clutched at his collar. Frederick coughed and the side of her face became studded with glistening rubies.

"We will see each other in heaven again."

"No, I don't want heaven," Abigail sobbed, barely able to see him through her tears. His eyes were dull. He was losing consciousness.

"I feel awful cold, Abi."

Abigail let out a scream from the bowels of the earth as the woodsman returned with the heavy horses.

Adulthood

The Early 1600s
Yorkshire
Northern England

It looked as though someone was painting streaks of red, pink and crimson across the sky. Coloured light was filtering through gaps between the clouds, flashing over the horizon and out of sight. There was a cold wind to wake her that morning, a sound like the reverse of the sea, or what she imagined the sea would be. For Abigail Craister had never been to the coast.

The wind buffeted through the heather, a shrill whistle by her ear as it swept over the top of her aching face. Her eyes hurt. The one she was looking out was weeping. She didn't know if it was weeping blood, tears or pus but she didn't care. Perhaps it was just the thick night dew that coated the rest of her dullened flesh. Her other eye, the left, had swollen shut overnight and she could only view a slit of light between encrusted lashes. She no longer had her cap. There was a bruise line at the top of her neck where the ties had been pulled. Some of her hair was still plaited, the rest hung blood-caked and limp around her bruised face. She let out a sigh and felt the pain in the side of her face. Perhaps her jaw had been fractured. Her hands were still balled as fists by her side, one holding the tooth that had come loose.

She lay and watched as the dawn swelled upon the sky and the world brightened. Time did not have meaning. She could not remember when she had ever been at liberty to simply lay back and stare at the sky. There was nothing to be done. No one calling for her. Very few would be concerned as to where she might be.

Eventually she sat up and looked about her surroundings. She was inside the sanctuary of the old stone circle on the moors. Rough, weather-driven furrows and lichen encrusted old rocks. No one really knew who had put them here. No, most didn't realise they even existed. This circle was away from any of the main moorland thorough ways.

Getting to her feet, Abigail waded across uneven ground, heather knee-deep, to squat outside of the circle and take a piss and a shit. She left the circle, not entering again but walking around the edge before starting her dry-mouthed trek over moorland.

Her grandmother had aged greatly since retreating to Chequers Farm on the hills above Osmotherley. She struggled to get out of her fireside chair when Abigail entered the kitchen. The wretch who appeared did not resemble her granddaughter, but her aura was the same. She would know that girl even if she were blind and deaf.

"Girl, my girl, what has happened to you?"

Abigail slumped down at the kitchen table. The farmer's wife looked uncertainly at the top of the girl's head. "I thought it might be your Abigail."

"Aye, and yet no," the old woman got herself up out of the chair and hobbled to the table, her stick thumping heavily on the floor. "What has happened to you?"

Abigail stared at her, a little glazed, but did not speak.

"I reckon you need something to eat and drink," the farmer's wife said, setting a small mug of weak beer before the girl. "I'll fetch you a drop of broth and bread. Perhaps a drop of spring water."

Picking up the mug, and putting it to her swollen lips, she realised this was not going to be a simple exercise. She had to pour it down her throat, misjudging the speed and having a gurgle of beer gush down her chin. No matter, her parched throat welcomed the drink.

Her grandmother sat down at the opposite side of the table to her, reaching out with a gnarled, arthritic hand of protruding knuckles and took Abigail's chin in her fingers. She turned the girl's head, ignoring the wince, to better see the swelling and bruises. She had been beaten about the head. "What has happened to you?"

Abigail remained mute. She looked down to the warm broth that had just been placed before her.

"I was sorry to hear of what happened to your betrothed. I am sorry I could not come to you. My legs seized last winter and I do not manage to get far. I sent word to Mrs Cook. Did you hear? It was a terrible, tragic accident."

"It was no accident," Abigail cut her short, the strength of her voice surprising everyone in the kitchen.

"No accident?" the old woman sounded confused. "I was told he was crushed by a great oak."

"The trunk was pushed into him. The props had been pulled out."

Words failed her. The old woman of Wass looked at her hands. She had heard of the betrothal, had been told about Frederick Flintoff. He had been a hardworking, good honest lad, with a positive mindset who had not let hardship or misfortune hold him back. Why, look what a carpenter he had become, and him with that shrivelled deformed arm he had carried with him like a penance from the day he was born. Who would want to hurt a cripple? "Did you go to the law about this? The magistrate? The squire of Kilburn?"

Abigail stared levelly at her, unblinking but said nothing. The two women held one another's stares, and they both understood. Just as when Abigail had been stumbling through the forest that awful day, and had come across her lord and master, Squire Angehard, with his blister-roughened muddy hands, suddenly sore from manual labour. He had a belligerent look about him, the arrogant child who knew he had done wrong but would never admit responsibility or guilt to anyone, even himself. A hot flush had rushed up his face when he saw that she had realised.

There had been too many people in the forest that day, too much drama already. He had stared down her glares, and remained haughtily ineffectual as she had hurried away from him. It had taken him over a week to find a moment to catch her own her own. He would leave his mark on her, in her, brand her of Kilburn. But the stupid wench had found back. She was stronger than he had expected, and he had gone all into the fight, punching her in the eye and taking her by the shoulders to slam her head into the corner of a wall. He'd flung her to the floor like a fistful of rags and pissed on her. Dirty, ugly wretch. What mesmerism had she put on him to make him think he might want her? The foul stench from her body brought forth vomit. No man in his right mind would want such an evil looking thing as a bed fellow. It was no wonder she'd been obligated to pursue a cripple. She was as misformed as she was repulsive.

Abigail slowly ate the food. Fingers like the busy legs of a spinning spider, ripping the bread into tiny chunks and soaking up the broth so she might easier eat. The granddaughter and grandmother did not try to speak anymore. The farmer's wife prepared a bundle of some food things. A metal mug the girl might use for water. She sensed Abigail Craister would not be returning to any house.

Abigail accepted the cloth bundle with a brief nod of thanks. She looked at her grandmother. "Don't try to follow me," she advised. Then she was gone.

The next weeks passed in a feverish blur. Abigail lost so much weight she grew shrunken and skeletal. She got an infection in her jaw, which swelled her face and formed an abscess that forced itself out of her lower cheek. It was a hot furious rod of pulsating foulness that funnelled up through her flesh to erupt out of her face. When the thing finally burned itself out and the skin healed up, she was left with a large shrunken scar, pitted and red like a burn on her face, and an indent in her jaw where some of the bone had dissolved away with the infection. Her body lacked in nutrients, and grew old before its time. Joints swelled and ached with the damp cold. Her hair tangled and matted like a sheet of felt, but she did not care to brush it out.

Abigail was in her cave on Black Hambleton Hill. Was it a cave or merely a grope into the earth? It did not go far into the hill, certainly not far enough to find the fairies, but it was enough that she could be out of the wind and the rain. It was wide enough that she could lay full length at the back on a few bushels of heather she had cut, and stare dumbly at the embers of the fire she occasionally thought to light. Sometimes she sobbed and screamed, ripped at her hair or her giddy fingers, at the sheer frustration that her dear heart had gone. He was lost, all for the unnecessary want of a delusional man who was no better than any other who walked the earth. Why was it that others got to marry their sweethearts, even those girls that were stolen away and raped, but Abigail Craister, who could go by her own name now that she was a troglodyte, got nothing in life. Oh Frederick, my own darling, you were too kind, too good for this world, and you were crushed out of it. Why could they not have been together when that devil shoved the tree down the bank? She would rather have died there than be left in this numbing limbo. They could have been crushed and mingled, blood seeping into blood, and at least she could have been where she belonged.

Out in the wider world rumours and gossip flew like wild bees. Mrs Cook fretted as to where Abigail-Mary had gone and what might have happened to her. Her nightmares were demonic as her suspicions grew and cemented over what had been going on up at the hermitage. She even walked to the Craister family home in Coxwold to see if the young woman might have fled there. The father could barely remember a scrappy, chestnut-haired little child of his first marriage. Abigail had been sent off into service a long time ago, he said. The wife, the new one, did not so much as want to admit such a person existed. She wanted nothing to do with the offspring of a witch, and had encouraged the others to move on a long time ago. But the offspring of a witch who might have been involved in murder, so some of the more malicious tongues suggested, no, such a she-devil was not welcome in Coxwold.

The old woodsman shook his head when he heard nonsense suggested that the girl might have killed her betrothed. He had been at the scene soon after and had the girl even wished it, she could not have shifted that tree. Ah, but her mother had been a witch, executed at the York assizes, don't you know, the sourest of the housewives whispered amongst themselves. And she must have fallen under the influence of that wicked Martha up at the hall at some time. The squire did nothing to discourage such chatter about his former employee. Rumours sourced from nowhere said she was a she-devil and a man hater. Why else would she chase after a cripple? After his arm for her witchcraft, but the squire had chased her away from her wicked intention. He had seen it all. The woodsman wondered why the squire had not intervened had he been present at the time. And why he had not been there when the crew had returned with the heavy horses. Why it was only Abigail that grieved. Her own grandmother heard the stories, told by a woman from down in Osmotherley village, who shook her head gravely and said there were enough hushed stories about over how badly young female maids were treated at Kilburn and that the decent folk knew that Abigail was a good girl. But no one could stand up and declare this, to offer Abigail sanctuary, and it grieved her grandmother that she was now completely outcast from society. Perhaps if she could have moved to another area, she could have started over, but that would require a benefactor. The longer Abigail was lost, the harder it was to think of a way to bring her back. And her grandmother was old and weary. The cruel world was beating her.

In her cave, in her nest of heather and grasses, feathers of lapwings and grouse, tufts of sheep fleece, Abigail slept more and more as her body weakened. She did not care. She simply no longer wished to be.

She woke one night, and ought to have been surprised by the healthy flickering fire, by the skinned rabbit on a spit, by the little pot of broth heating over the flames. The scent of roasting meat drifted across, sparking a reaction in her nostrils long since forgotten. The brightness of the dancing flames pushed the clear night stars to the background. Smoke twisted upwards and out of the cave opening. A figure moved, stepping through her field of vision, and crouched to check on the cooking for a moment. They stood up again, then paused, realising Abigail was awake, before shifting around the cave to sit on a hewn stump that they must have brought to the cave themselves, for Abigail had not seen it before. It was a woman, perhaps in her thirties, with loose wavy auburn hair and reddened hands. She hunched forward, resting her elbows on her knees, and peered at Abigail with a friendly countenance. Abigail looked at her and realised she knew her, although she struggled to place the face.

"It will soon be ready to eat," the woman said gently. "You must not give up hope. My dear girl, if it were not for the good folk like us, the world would be a devil of a place. You still have good to do." She dipped a cup in the broth then moved closer, gently stroking Abigail's forehead before helping her to sit up. "Drink."

They sat in silence side by side for a time, watching the fire dance. Abigail finished the broth, then looked back at the woman with a gasp of realisation. "Oh, Mamma,"

Her mother smiled and embraced her, a hand cradling the back of her head. She kissed her daughter on the crown of her head. "I am so proud of you."

Abigail started to cry, her eyes blurred by tears as she pushed her face into her mother's shoulder. "I have missed you so much," she whimpered. When she pulled back and wiped her eyes on her filthy sleeve, she was alone in the cave, the little cup at her feet and the rabbit crackling. It was time to eat.

Another night she woke to find her grandmother sitting on the stump at the side of the cave. It was a time before she spoke, watching Abigail with concern. "Remember the earth will care for you," she finally said. "When it's time, do not be afraid."

Abigail sat up and nodded, realising that her grandmother had just passed away in her sleep. She was gone. There was no one left in the world for her.

One morning she woke and realised it was deep winter. She pulled the ice crystals from her eyelashes, watched her breath steam out from the cave mouth as if it were home to a great dragon. With no sense of the future or self, she got up and began to make arrangements. She threw out all of the heather bushels and dry grass, burning it all so that the parasites would die in the flames. She gathered rocks and made a dry stone wall across a section of the cave entrance. The snow soon blew to cover it with white, and blend it with the rest of the landscape. The barrier kept the worst of the wind and rain out, but enough space for light and for smoke to escape. She dug down through the snow and cut fresh heather with her knife. Walked down to the woodland and gathered dead, frost-hardened bracken to take back up for her bedding. Boiled snow for water. Caught rabbits. Came back one day to find a folded woollen blanket with half a dozen eggs and a block of cheese. Folk knew she was there, although none would admit to it. They also knew that now her grandmother and mother were gone, Abigail was the one who would know how to help a woman out. The knowledge was in the blood. Others would have perished by now up there, but the land embraced those women. They would always be safe. And so, a woman who had lost everything, could find a way to exist.

In all the years she lived up on Black Hambleton, Frederick never visited her once. Abigail dreamt of him many times, but he was illusive, always out of grasp, and would never speak. In waking hours she would think of him even more. It started when she woke, when she sat at the edge with first light, listening to a curlew's call as it flew over the moorland tops. A haunting call that gave the endless stretch of the open horizon a mournful depth.

Abigail's face aged before its time. Her skin thickened and turned ruddy from the wind and the sun. The landscape of her profile was pitted from the scars of old disease and abscesses. Her hair was never brushed and grew matted, forming a warming shawl across her head and the back of her neck. Her feet were forever blistered with chilblains. Her joints ached in the cold, melted in the sun-kissed warmth of summers. She gathered herbs and boiled salves to ease the symptoms, but she would never return to the girl she had been before. She went weeks without speaking to a soul, and her outer voice grew quiet and granular. Her eyes grew canny. She watched the long lines of drovers and their cattle cross over the moors of Black Hambleton to avoid the tolls, on the ever onwards route to London. In the late summer the dogs would come running back on the paths alone, or walking with masters who could not afford the carriage fare back north. Or preferred to save for something greater.

The local women sought her help. It was a rare thing that they had to seek her out, for often Abigail would appear in the locality when she was going to be called upon. She stayed away from people and community, and folk would wonder afterwards how she lived out there in the wilds and how she kept herself. How didn't she freeze to death in the worst of the winters when they listened to the winds howl and the snow pelt against the farmhouse door? She wasn't seen for weeks, and folk would say this had been the winter to catch her. Then her shape would be seen on the horizon one day, shifting across snow crusted heather. She had great boots of willow frame and rabbit fur she had constructed herself that would get her across the snow drifts in safety. Always in the distance, in the background, never to engage in the regular comings and goings of folk.

At least until things stumbled into her path.

There was a time when Abigail was some distance away from her cave home. It was summer, and a dry one at that. She had a roll of supplies upon her back, and had sat down in a dip to rest. The green, lush bracken was crackling and unfurling high amongst the heather. The great fronds went to give her some shade from the sun. Abigail idly dug her fingers into the dry peaty earth, surprised even herself at how easily it parted and welcomed her. Like dust, and tinder dry. She took up a handful and brought it up to her squinting eyes. When the rains came, they would hit hard at this earth. Too much at once and it wouldn't be able to absorb it all. The water would rush on through until it hit a unyielding layer, and the floods would come.

A track climbed up the hillside, passing by a few yards across from where she rested. The path was paved here, great hewn blocks of stone which had been carted up, to make safe passage for folk during wetter times. This patch was apt to turn particularly boggy. Abigail was rather secluded but had a good view down a stretch of the path. She watched as a local farm lass appeared into view. She was walking alone, a basket of goods in the crook of her arm. Humming to herself and quite oblivious to her surroundings.

Enjoying the summer. There was another body somewhere, Abigail sensed, although she could not see it yet.

The third party soon made itself known. A figure descended the hill and blocked the path first with his shadow, then his body. He stood legs akimbo, hands on hips and elbows outwards so that he could physically fill the passage through the bracken forest. Passing by would be awkward at best. The girl slowed, a look of horror sinking upon her as she recognised the young man. A figure she had history with. The sense of being alone and far from folk lost its peace and folded outwards menacingly.

"Bess," the man spoke. "It's time you stopped this merry dance of denial. You've had your fun and it's time a man had his reward."

It was instinct that made her look around for help even though she knew she was alone. Abigail was disguised and blended into the undergrowth shadows, and remained unseen. Bess assessed the path ahead and realised she wasn't going to slip by. Placing her free hand, which was starting to shake, on the handle of her basket, she turned away to go back down the hill. "I have my chores to attend to. I will be missed."

"No you don't," he corrected her. He grabbed at her arm and wrenched her back. For a minute or two the pair of them wrestled over the basket as if it was a mere thieving of property he was about. He won over, sweeping the basket back out of her reach and flinging it out over the tops of the bracken. It disappeared into the greenery, the uncurled fronds catching it from the worst of impact with the ground.

"I know you lasses like to pretend to be shy," he spoke, now able to focus all his strength on forcing her up. "But it's futile to continue. You'll never be my wife, you're far beneath me..." the girl looked horrified at this notion. "... a man of my status'll do a lot better when that time comes. But you and I can have a little fun in the summer."

"I think not," Bess protested, trying to push him away. The vice of his arms only grew stronger. She wasn't a weak lass, for she worked hard on the farm and churned butter most days, but she could not compete with this. She'd felt the uncomfortable lick of his gaze whenever he'd been at the farm for months now, and had tried to keep out of his way. He'd caught her a few occasions, but always she'd been saved by someone coming. He'd been gone a few weeks, and perhaps she'd been a fool and relaxed and decided she might take a walk on her own. Look where this had got her now.

She let out a cry as he put his foot behind her ankle when she tried to pull away again. Losing her balance, he helped her to fall backwards into a springing, willing bed of bracken. She fought back as she found her skirts being flung up into her face, a rough hand shoved into her face to push her back down against the ground. She couldn't help but cry, even though she knew better than any that tears wouldn't help her. She threw her head back and screamed in distress when she felt his fingers running up the inside of her thigh.

There was a strange croak, like someone trying to speak having recovered from a long bout of influenza. He stopped to look for the interruption, and in the shift of his body, Bess could see a woman dressed in ragged clothing and no cap upon her head. At a glance a crone, but on closer inspection, not all that old, and she realised it was the infamous Abigail Craister.

The man laughed. "Getting jealous? I'd say I'd do you next except I'd be too afraid of catching the pox."

Bess took her chance in the distraction to wriggle free, slipping under his arm and away towards the path. He shouted in irritation and grabbed her around the waist. "Bugger back off to your toad hole, witch," he cursed at Abigal.

Abigail muttered something low. He swung around, low and growling, a predator hunkering over its next meal that it would not share. Abigail's hand flashed up and released what it had been holding. It seemed like a cloud, a chestnut storm that flashed in the sun then dispersed into the man's face. He let out a roar as the thing met his eyes, melting onto the damp surface of his eyeballs and stinging violently at the surface. Bess took her chance and pulled away, darting a few yards down the path, well out of reach.

"Blessings on you, Abigail Craister!" she called out.

"Your basket," Abigail spoke hoarsely.

"You find it, you keep it," Bess called over her shoulder as she ran down the path. "I'll not stay here a second longer. My thanks for your help."

"Evil bitches!" the man shrieked, scratching at his eyes to clear his vision. He only made it worse. His eyes streamed with salt. His vision was clouded and blurred, shimmerings of copper and senses of light and shadow. "I'll catch you for this, you witch!" he threatened the hag, blindly reaching out to try and pull her down.

Abigail had already disappeared from view, slipping into gaps between the bracken to retrieve the basket. The young man could see to himself.

The weeping sore on his thigh had started to throb every time the horse's hooves thundered back down on the earth. Montague Angehard pushed the thought of the pain down. That thing had been pustulating on his leg for a couple of months, and just now there was more important quarry to be had. It would shut up that pompous old fart about his son's eyes, but more importantly it could put an end to two years of nightmares for Montague. If the witch was rooted out, she would not be able to pour bile into his mind at night.

He could vaguely hear his neighbour, some distance behind him, shout. The meaning and the words were lost to noise of the galloping horses. The baying of the hounds bounded towards them. Whatever that twerp yelled, it wouldn't be important. He already knew that the son had fallen from his horse. He'd be all right, the clumsy clot had toppled off into heather. They would blame it on the loss of sight in one eye, as if the lad had never been born a fool. It hadn't been surprising when they'd first heard of the attack which had led to the eye infection. Only a clot like he would try to seduce a maid and end up with dirt in his eyes, screaming and sobbing for his mother that he had been made blind. It had taken weeks to clear up, indeed it had looked a mess when Montague had seen him. And one eye never did see properly again.

"The stupid boy has a notion he won't get his sight back until he marries the lass," the father had bemoaned at him at one of the suppers of the local gentry. "Some common dairy slut to boot," he'd continued, slurping his wine. "I say that dirt diseased more than his eye. A dalliance I could forgive, a man has to sow his young oats, but he needs to remember these people are little better than the cattle. It's a bewitchment, I tell you."

"You suspect witchcraft?"

"Oh indeed."

"Have you located the maid?"

"No, it wasn't her. She was a mere tease. My lad tells me there was a hag on the moors casting mischief in his eye. I have heard tell of her, she lives up there on the moors in her own filth. Poaching. Causing trouble for me. Craister, they call her. Well, she killed a cripple on your land I hear."

"A cripple on my land?" His brow creased. He had not been informed of this.

"A year or two ago now. He was crushed by a tree."

Knocking and wrenching the stocks from the ground.

"What did you say the hag's name was?"

"Craister," the man belched. "Abigail Craister. The commoners go to her for help. Help I say, and look what she did to my boy. It can't be allowed to continue."

He closed his eyes and slowly set his glass on the table. A memory of chestnut curls flashed up. A frustration in his veins. He had punched that beauty out of her face and yet she still haunted him. He could never win over her. "I worry," he began, "that we have grown lax since the successes of my father. We rooted out the witches then, I aided him. But I fear the devil's kin have returned."

"No doubt about it."

"We need another purge."

They had not planned it this way. They had been out on the hill tops above Kilburn – anything than to have to sit in the hall and listen to that fool drone on – and were exercising the horses and the hounds. A figure on the distant line who could have easily been ignored. Except they were all restless and tired of being inert indoors, and the lad had pointed and shouted out her name. Frustration at his own failure that still followed him two steps behind reared up in his blood. Silently, collectively they had understood what they were about now. Even the master of the hounds, the staff, not privy to all the drunken complaints of the gentry, seemed to sense that things had shifted. Most were hardened men used to the harsh brutality of nature. A couple of the beaters, local men, had slunk off in the background and disappeared down the hill to the woods. They would not stop it but neither would they take part.

The moment he saw that she realised what was afoot, he felt the anticipation of conquest. It bubbled through his blood, almost making him giddy. He was more in control than he had felt for months. She'd been carrying a bundle of what looked like twigs, which she swiftly dropped and leapt, deer-like, over the heather. She was a scrawny thing, a gathering of flapping rags like a destitute crow. There was no decency about her, no cap or even her hair tied back. It flew out behind her like a chestnut cape.

It was strange for Abigail to feel her heightened pulse and fast breathing. To see how her eyes darted to each direction, and her brain overtook her numbed stance. She was searching for cover. She was reverting to animal instinct, a hunted creature who needed to get away. She hadn't felt much in recent years, once the grief for Frederick had dropped to an anesthetised acceptance. Perhaps not even that, she had simply shut down. A sheep didn't mourn its dead lamb that long. Animals moved on. Abigail was isolated, she didn't speak, she was less human and more beast. She had lived this way for so long that she had neglected the politics of men, or that the weak-minded and afflicted could carry a grudge till the death. She had grown lazy and over confident in her right to exist wild on the moors around Black Hambleton.

She'd been out cutting fresh heather on the moorland that morning. There had been quite the bundle tied up on her back when they'd found her, something she had instinctively dropped and abandoned. Things will only hold you back. She'd wandered too far from her safe places. From the stone circle, from her cave, from the acres of moorland she knew so intimately that every hillock, every dip in the topography, was ingrained on her subconsciousness. She'd roamed today, perhaps thinking of happier times, perhaps being drawn back in the direction of home.

She'd forgotten all about the young rapist whom she'd flung dirt in his eyes. Worse, she hadn't thought of her old master and how his need for dominance, and failure over her, would be an oozing, seeping wound. Hidden with bravado and cruelty in front of society, but it was there, a secret thing. Even in that distance, when she hadn't been able to clearly see the horseriders' features, she had known who they were.

A bloom of sweet heather scent, inappropriate for the chase, curled up her nostrils as she dropped into a dip, submerging herself in the scratching heather and disappearing completely from sight. The sounds of the hounds baying was ominous thunder on the horizon. The dogs hadn't been fed for days and they were angry, angry and desperate to be fed. And in that dog like way, they were so keen to make the master proud, and the pack triumphant. Perhaps then they would be treated better.

There was a pungent, earthy scent lingering, and for a moment she wondered if she had unknowingly soiled herself. No, despite all that had happened, she had always kept a calm inner control. She glanced across, and saw a fox hunkered down in the heather close by. Foxes knew how hounds dreamt of them, rendering flesh apart, howling with blood splattered muzzles to the sky. It was a knowledge they were born with. She could have told herself that they were out after the fox, but she knew it was not true. For a moment the fox looked directly at her, and silently the two appraised one another.

The fox darted away and Abigail cried out, her voice weak and rasping. Her hand went to try and grab at the animal, but it had been too quick and was already gone. It knew that they did not want his blood today, but it was not naïve enough either to think it would be ignored. It was too great a risk, but it had been taken.

Further out on the moors, their attention was caught by sudden movement, as a fox, brilliant chestnut in the sun, a flash of white tipped tail, appeared from the cover of the heather. It ran out onto patchy grassland, darting and curving, looking to loop around the hunting party and away. The horses snorted, expecting a chase, but they were reigned in. The hounds, whose pack instinct could overtake command at times, let rip in a collective howl and chased after the fox. Their masters shouted and cursed, but they would not listen. Abigail had raised herself on her forearms to be able to peer over the heather tops. She could see the gift that had been offered. It would be her only chance to get away whilst the distraction diverted the party's attention.

Montague felt his horse go to rear and reigned it in. Stamping and pacing on the spot, the riders were in a twist of confusion. The hound master had run off after the damned dogs. "Get them rounded up and back, damned beasts!" he roared. Father and son looked confused for a moment, then fearful when they thought perhaps this squire was serious about hunting down and killing another person. Of course there were rumours and hushed stories that his was not a good home to be an employee in, especially if one was a woman. But then witches were a scourge of the earth and needed removing. Arresting and taken to court, was that not the way? The father looked as though he was about to protest, but changed his mind. Bringing his horse around, he and his son rode off to bring the pack back in line.

Montague's horse was brought full circle on the spot. He saw the witch hag seemingly appear out of the air, rising like a foul mist from the heather. She had seen her chance and would get away from them. The last time he had seen her he had beaten her so that her head had cracked. Yet she remained defiant. Her existence, her sheer gall to interfere and attack another man, why it could not be allowed. It was a stain on his authority. His status. He was alone and without hounds, but he could take her and finish her. He kicked the horse into action.

Abigail had never run so quickly, nor been so nimble in leaping over the hillocks of rough moorland shrubs that were scattering more and more to a patchwork of grasslands and scrub, bilberry and bracken joining the mix. Her heart seemingly pounded in her ears, her breathing so intense that there was no space to think, only to flee and hope that cover would appear soon. A forest where she could get lost, or better, a hole that could break a horse's leg. She knew he was following her. The fox had distracted the others, but he was following.

She had not been thinking. Had she been calm and numb, she would have considered her route, but fresh unaccustomed panic had done her wrong. She gasped as she came stumbling out towards the cliff edge, realising where she was, and that she had cut off potential escape routes. Not only was she exposed here with no cover, but there was no going forward. The steep, sharp cliffs of white stone dropped down into steeply wooded banks, littered with aged rock fall and broken branches. Beyond was the still and silent glittering surface of Lake Gormire. The small freshwater pool submerged with lore of sunken villages. Overshadowed by Hood Hill.

She turned away and ran to her left a little way, skimming the edge of the cliffs, before the sound of the horse snorting alerted her that her options had been cut short. Gasping for breath, she stopped and turned inland as it were, to see her old Lord astride his horse, glaring at her as if he had met the very devil. She had the brazen nerve to meet his eye, staring out from the tangled mess of hair that fell about her face. For a moment or two she looked like the young maid in fresh bloom he remembered from the hall. Then the breeze picked up and brushed the hair from her face and he saw the scarring, the damage of a broken jaw and infections. This is what happened when a woman left the security of his household.

They were silent. Regarding one another. Abigail flicked her eyes left, then right, and understood he would cut her off if she chose either. It was time to stop running and draw a line in the sand. This was how it would be.

"Witch," he hissed.

The insult didn't hurt. She almost wished she was what he called her, for if the nonsense tales they told one another in the firelight at night were true, she ought to be able to morph into a hare and run away, or kick her heels together and fly away to the clouds or wave her arms about muttering incantations and evoke the devil who would devour him and his horse in return for some debauched intercourse on a hill or a church roof or wherever the depraved believed such things happened.

She took a few steps back and gingerly twisted to look over her shoulder. It was a long way down. The safe splash of the lake was far, far out of reach or leap.

"There is nowhere to go now." He wondered if he ought to take his sword and run her through. Rid the earth of her poison. Now there were no witnesses, he wasn't sure if he had the courage to do it. "You will be tried for witchcraft for blinding that boy..."

Ah, so it was about the dirt in the eyes. That privileged young man. A trifle to Abigail. They knew it wasn't about the boy.

"I will watch you burn."

Even yet she was silent. The bitch would not speak to him. "Speak, whore of Satan!"

Silence.

He wanted her on her knees. Tear stained and snot bubbling from her nostrils. Begging for forgiveness. Admitting her faults. Seeing the wisdom and the greatness that he was. That she had been such a lucky girl that he had taken note of her, and she had been stupid and resisted. He wanted to hear her say that he was right.

Silence.

Abigail had a choice. Two choices. Neither were pleasant. She looked again to the cliffs, then back to the weak man on a horse. He proffered a hand as if asking a lady up. Whore of Satan indeed. She'd tell him he'd rot in hell, only there was no such place. How foolish to spend a life running from the threat of a place that never existed. Two choices. No one had ever promised eternal life, other than the reverend bleating of heaven and hell. That's not where we went, and we all had to go sometime. Frederick had been lost from her all these weeks and months and days and seconds and years. Perhaps she was already lost to herself.

His eyes widened as the girl, without a word, turned and jumped off the cliff. The moment of her in the air, the sunlight lighting up her chestnut hair and her torn, filthy rags, remained in his mind until the day of his death, years from that day. Then she was gone. No scream, no cry. A crack of branches, thrashing of leaves and the heavy plummet. Smashed on a boulder. Absorbed by the tree canopy. When he looked over the edge of the cliff, there was nothing to be seen. Silver birches had springing branches. Trees would stand strong against any projectile. On the forest floor Abigail was splashed with dirt. Mingled with blood, which seeped and poured from a cracked skull. Leg bent at an unnatural angle. Shattered bone protruding from skin. Arm flung out, fingers stretched and almost digging into the earth as one last escape. Warm blood ran down the length of her arm and dispersed into the soil. Iron nourishing the ground.

And so was the end of Abigail Craister. As news, shaky and uncertain, got about, other stories joined the confusion of the end of Frederick. Of the myths of Gormire, and how it was bottomless, or perhaps there was a sinkhole and it came up, miles away in a freshwater spring. Someone said they'd seen Abigail walking on a path up from the lake. Another said she'd been riding her broomstick over Coxwold. Everyone heard that she had been a witch, well, her mother had been executed for it, and there had always been something odd about that grandmother. And if she would fly, a jump from those high cliffs would have easily seen her drop into the lake, safely cushioned by the waters' depths. Some women had a coy smile on their lips as they recounted the stories. The squire never did get the better of Abigail Craister. She got away, down that sink hole and away to live in peace. To walk the forests as she wished.

Now hush children and settle in to bed, or else Abigail Craister might catch up with you. And would that be a bad thing if she did? Maisie lent back and pursed her lips, the contours of her face illuminated by candle light. I doubt it. Abigail Craister never did anyone any harm.

Historical Note

The Witch of Gormire is a work of fiction, and all the characters and events are fiction. Yes, there is an element of folklore inspiration here, but essentially the only character you could say is real is the landscape itself. The places existed and still do, the people do not.

Abigail Craister exists in something of a grey zone. This all started with a few vague folk stories of a witch named Abigail Craister. Not even the bare bones of a real person, so she is very much a product of imagination. And Abigail is one of the witches who is rapidly being forgotten, for she often doesn't appear in books about Yorkshire witches, and tales from North Yorkshire.

I actually first came across her name when I was reading an old guide to The Cleveland Way, that long distance walking route from Helmsley to Filey that takes in moorland before swinging around to the coast. I'd picked up the guide second hand and it is decades old, published long before the age of glossy colour photos and OS map pages showing every meter of the walk. In this guide there's as much about the history and folklore of the region as there is about the route you're going to walk. Bill Cowley (yes, he of the Lyke Wake Walk) wrote the guide in the 1970s and mentions it was a cobbler from South Kilvington who told him about Abigail. Prior to that, it had been one of those eager reverends of the 1800s who seemed to do everything but preach, George Calvert, who had collected folk tales, including Abigail, in the early 1800s. Cowley mentions this "witch-hag" who lived in a cave on Black Hambleton and had great knowledge, and power over "rattens and coneyes". Two tales of her deeds are mentioned; once when her rattens dug into the foundations of a building of a terrible priest, who had hidden a damsel there with intentions to ravish her. The other tale is of a girl pursued by the squire's son, a lad who clearly couldn't take no for an answer. He followed her up to the moors and would have had his way, were it not for a sudden pain in his eyes, and he was blinded. Apparently Abigail did that. It seems Abigail Craister was the hero of women under attack from randy, disrespectful men.

In the guide Cowley also mentions a tale of a local witch who was chased by hounds and flung herself from Whitestone cliffs into Gormire. Lucky woman actually reached the water, went into a sinkhole at the bottom and popped out of a spring some miles from the lake.

A lot of other books on the area never mention her, so gleaning anymore information was hard, to impossible. Peter N Walker did mention her a little in his books, telling of a tale from the reign of James I (he reigned from 1603 - 1625) when an Abigail Glaister as he calls her, was suspected of witchcraft and was killed when she leapt from Whitestone Cliff. His daughter, Sarah Walker has also mentioned Abigail in her blog, writing about a ghost seen by folk driving about the Sutton Bank area. Abigail also gets a short mention in the excellent *Folklore of Yorkshire* by Kai Roberts, again mentioning the hounds, the cliff and the escape from Gormire. And that her ghost haunts the area, riding her broomstick over Kilburn.

It's not really much to go on. But the story stuck with me, and every time I am up on Sutton Bank walking past that view of Lake Gormire down below, I shake my head and think, there's no way anyone could jump that far. Admittedly the landscape would have been a little different in the 1600s to what we see now. There have been rockfalls from Whitestone Cliff since that era. In the 1600s the cliffs would have stuck further out than they do today. But not that much so that a person could leap from the cliff and land in the lake. There's a long steep wooded slope between the cliff and the still, silent lake. Anyone jumping is going to have a rough ride down to earth through the trees and onto the rock fall on the forest floor.

So, who might Abigail Craister have been? Indeed, who was any witch? Cowley mentions a witch hag, but no woman is born a hag living in isolation in a cave. She came from somewhere. Furthermore, I am tired by the old rhetoric of these old ugly witches. It's something that still persists, even today when recounting these old stories. Even last year (2024), I went to an interesting exhibition on old folk charms and remedies against witchcraft, and in the collected articles in an accompanying book, it was written how these women were ugly.

Were they even ugly? Does it even matter? Well, they may well have been ugly by today's concepts of beauty, but the question has to be, were the women not accused of witchcraft anymore attractive? These were not easy times to live in, with parasites and scaring from childhood disease, no central heating, malnutrition and hard living. Perhaps the entire community looked a bit rough. But why does it matter and why is it the women that are focused on this way? When you read about the men of folklore, the wise men and other figures, you generally never heard about their appearance for better or worse. As if it's irrelevant.

Well, of course we're not so naïve as to not realise that a woman's looks have always been culturally important, to the point of being the sole defining feature of a woman's person. In the cautionary fairytales, it was always a story telling device to show purity and goodness against the evils of this world. But here's the thing. The victors write history. And how do you damage a woman's name and belittle her? It still goes on, even today. And I'm sure we've all heard the little scorned man who was rejected trying to soothe his ego. She's ugly, she's frigid, she's worthless because she turned me down. And it saddens me to see this rhetoric continuing in writing about witches and actual characters from the locality being described in this way. Still using the misogynistic belittling terminology. Because the witch trials and persecution were all about misogyny. You only need to read a bit of *Malleus Maleficarum* to feel the hate for all women kind.

So who were these women in actuality? As real, living people? Where did they grow up, how did they live and how did it come to be that we half remember their names and the strange stories tied to them? This is what I have been pondering on, and as the fascination with these snippets of Abigail Craister grew, I decided I wanted to have a go at writing my own imagined tale of her life.

All the books in the Yorkshire Saga find inspiration in folklore and local history. I read all sorts, too much detail to put into the stories, so I have a blog running alongside where I write about the background. If you find yourself curious, take a look:

https://yorkshiresaga.wordpress.com/

Cowley, Bill, The Cleveland Way, 1977 4ed, The Dalesman Publishing Company Ltd

Walker, Peter. N., Murders and Mysteries from the North York Moors, 1988, Robert Hale Ltd

Roberts, Kai, Folklore of Yorkshire, 2013, The History Press

Walker, Sarah, The Countryman's Daughter Blog
https://countrymansdaughter.com/

www.ingramcontent.com/pod-product-compliance
Lightning Source LLC
LaVergne TN
LVHW050935080826
845145LV00004B/1268